Also by Maleeha Siddiqui

Barakah Beats

MALEEHA SIDDIQUI

BHAI FOR NOW

SCHOLASTIC PRESS
NEW YORK

All rights reserved. Published by Scholastic Press, an imprint of Scholastic Inc., *Publishers since 1920*. SCHOLASTIC, SCHOLASTIC PRESS, and associated logos are trademarks and/or registered trademarks of Scholastic Inc.

The publisher does not have any control over and does not assume any responsibility for author or third-party websites or their content.

Library of Congress Cataloging-in-Publication Data available

ISBN 978-1-338-70209-5

1 2022

Printed in the U.S.A.   23

First edition, October 2022

Book design by Omou Barry

For my brothers. May you always be
each other's best friends.

1
SHAHEER

Shaheer threw an armload of clothes onto the bed of his fourth bedroom in four years and kicked the empty box out into the hallway. He couldn't stand the smell of cardboard. Maybe if his life wasn't like a train that barely stopped long enough to let people on and off, he wouldn't hate it as much. At least he wouldn't be around it all the freakin' time.

"Ah, someone finally decided to unpack," Dad said, appearing in the doorway with a mug of chai.

"Look who's talking. You live out of a suitcase," Shaheer deadpanned.

"Not anymore. I hung my clothes up," Dad said proudly. "On real hangers."

Shaheer rolled his eyes. He didn't see the point in

1

setting up his room, and it wasn't like he had a lot of stuff anyway. None of them did. Their next destination was always on the horizon. It was inevitable, like getting half a cheese slice on a McDonald's fish filet sandwich. Their time in every city ended with them saying goodbye, and this spot in Northern Virginia would be next. Shaheer knew they were only going to be there temporarily, no matter what lies Dad fed him about this being "it." As if. Shaheer might believe it if he, Dad, and Dada slept on real beds instead of mattresses, put up curtains for once, and didn't eat off disposable plates all the time.

Dad sipped his chai and peered at Shaheer over the mug's rim. "You excited for school tomorrow?"

Shaheer gave Dad a *What do you think?* look. After years of hopping around from school to school, he'd learned it was easier to hold back and roll with the punches. He almost forgot what it was like to put his feelings into words. Shaheer let his silence do all the talking now.

"Do me a favor, sport?" Dad said. "Please try to get involved this time. Make friends. Join a club. Go to the masjid."

The *masjid*? When was the last time Shaheer had set foot in one? Did this have something to do with how he'd thrown a fit the whole month of Ramadan? Shaheer technically should have fasted more than the seven days his dad and grandfather had managed to crank out of him. But it wasn't like Dad prayed five times a day or anything. In fact, Shaheer was pretty sure he didn't even attend Friday prayers regularly. If Dad wanted him to do those things, then *he* should try doing them himself first.

Instead, Dad spent all his energy chasing the next shiny hospital job like it was a pot of gold at the end of a rainbow. Shaheer had no clue what Dad got out of it.

"What do you say?" Dad asked, continuing the one-way conversation. Shaheer brushed past him to the kitchen of the three-bedroom apartment.

"Sure. Whatever," said Shaheer. He pretended to search for a snack, but the only thing he could find was leftover salad that came with the gyros they'd had for lunch. It was all soggy, but Dada refused to throw food away unless it'd gone beyond bad. Well, someone had to eat it, and Shaheer didn't feel like going back to the room that would never be *his*, or give Dad the chance to keep talking to him. He took up the plate of salad, grabbed a disposable fork, and flopped down on Dada's favorite armchair in the living room near where his grandfather was making dua.

Shaheer chewed on a limp piece of lettuce as he waited for his grandfather to finish praying. When Dada finally looked up from his splayed hands, Shaheer asked him, "What do you ask so hard for?" Dada took so long making dua that sometimes Shaheer had to poke him to make sure he was still alive.

"Oh, you know," he said wistfully. Dada sounded younger than sixty-four. He was like a sturdy, uncracked beam that could still hold up the whole house. "Jannah for your dadi. Health. A full head of hair. Hey, we're supposed to believe in miracles!" he exclaimed when Shaheer smirked. "We'll see who gets the last laugh when, God willing, you get to my age."

Shaheer smoothed back his hair fondly. It had grown out longer than it'd ever been and started curling at the nape of his neck and falling into his eyes. His hair was the only thing about his appearance he liked, and the thought of it falling out made him feel faint.

"Way to scare him, Abba," Dad piped up. He was sitting with his legs crossed against the wall dividing the kitchen from the living room. That wall, Shaheer thought, was a waste of space. It could be taken out and replaced with an island so that the place looked more open. This apartment was nicer than some of the others they'd lived in, but it didn't get the Property Brothers' seal of approval.

Shaheer had had no clue what "open concept" or "clean lines" meant until a few years ago when they were stuck inside the house for months during a global pandemic. At one point, Dad stayed at the hospital for a whole month to care for patients in the ER and to avoid bringing the virus home, especially since Dada was high risk. That was when Dada morphed into a devout HGTV watcher to distract himself from worrying about Dad. Shaheer had never been so happy to see Dad as the day when he finally came home. That was back when the two of them were still tight.

Shaheer didn't get Dada's interior design obsession at first, but when he started joining him out of sheer boredom, he suddenly started noticing how subtle transformations lit up people's faces. How the way a house changed to suit a particular family's needs suddenly made it a *home*. Shaheer thought it was cool that the twins on *Property Brothers* worked together. He didn't have siblings or a Forever Home. Shaheer might never have either of those things at this rate, so he had to settle for being happy for others who did.

"What are you eating?" Dada asked, peering at Shaheer's plate.

"The day's special," said Shaheer, thrusting a piece of tomato into his mouth.

"Why didn't you tell me you were hungry?" Dad said. "I would've ordered us pizza."

"No, no. We've eaten out too much these last few days. It's time I made us a real dinner," Dada said. "Jawad, did you unbox the masala jars? You did the groceries yesterday, right? Great. Here, give me this." Dada took the sad-looking salad out of Shaheer's hands. "I'll finish it. How about I make you anda salan?"

Shaheer sat up. Anda salan was egg curry with cut-up potatoes tossed in. It was the most basic of basic Pakistani dishes, and one of the few things Dada knew how to cook. Shaheer, who rarely got homemade meals, thought it was delicious. And he liked knowing that Dada had gotten the recipe from Shaheer's mom years ago.

Shaheer had never met his mom. His parents had divorced when he was a baby. He didn't know much besides her name because the one time he'd been curious about her, Dad shut him down. Hard. Made it clear the topic was off-limits. He'd been happier to answer Shaheer's burning questions about puberty when he was ten.

Shaheer had never even seen a picture of his mom. When he thought about it, it wasn't normal. No pictures of someone his dad had supposedly loved enough to marry and have a kid with?

As Dada headed toward the kitchen, Shaheer scampered to retrieve their one giant pot in the lower kitchen cabinet and put it on the stove himself before Dada could. Dada had back problems and wasn't allowed to bend over a lot. Shaheer always made sure Dada wasn't doing anything that could get himself hurt, even though it made Dada grumble about not being *that* old. Like now. He muttered to himself as he boiled eggs with his reading glasses sitting atop his head.

"Really, Abba. I could've had something delivered. You don't have to stand for so long," Dad said.

"Bah," Dada said, waving him off. "Not that old yet. My feet are fine. So are yours, Dr. Atique. Put 'em to good use and add some rice to the cooker. Shaheer, get me a tomato and one potato, please. Now, what were you two talking about earlier? Allah forgive me, I was listening while reading namaz."

"Oh, I was telling Shaheer that he should do some kind of activity. Remember how many extracurriculars I used to do in school?" Dad said, measuring out a cup of rice.

"That's 'cuz you were a show-off," Dada said in Urdu. Shaheer pressed his lips together to keep from grinning.

"But don't you think it's true?" Dad asked. "It'd be better than coming straight home every day." Dad was a total wanderer. When he wasn't working, he loved to get out of the house and explore new places or try new things. Shaheer stopped joining Dad two moves ago out of defiance. What was the point in getting to know a place you'd just leave behind?

"He lives like this because you refuse to give the boy a chance to make a life somewhere." Leave it to Dada to not beat around the bush.

"What about a sport?" Dad said like he hadn't heard him. "Or volunteer work."

"Shaheer's not you, Jawad," Dada said gently. "Let him decide for himself."

Dad's eyebrows pinched in Dada's direction, his hand going still over the rice cooker. "What's that supposed to mean? I'm not allowed to give my own son advice?"

"Yes, I'm well aware he's *your* son, thanks," said Dada.

Shaheer sighed, watching Dada slice the tomato with a little too much force. Honestly, what was their deal? Dad and Dada were almost always fine. Then at random times certain comments unleashed some old feud and they never clued Shaheer in. Shaheer was used to it, and it was usually the perfect distraction for him when he wanted to be alone, but the bad mojo lingered in the air for too long afterward.

Dad muttered something about Dada never taking his side and moved to the sink to soak the rice.

"He's always been restless," Dada whispered to Shaheer. "Hard for him to stay in one place for too long. You should say something to him about it, too, you know. He never listens to me, not since he was a kid. Not even when—" Dada stopped short and got this faraway look in his eyes. It happened sometimes, Dada's mood shifting out of the blue, and Shaheer never understood why. There was no way Dad thought Shaheer liked all the moving around. If he couldn't see something so obvious, then what was the point in *telling* him?

"Anyway," Dada continued as he cut the potato into squares. "It's not a bad idea. Maybe a recreational activity is what you need." Shaheer's forehead crinkled. "Not saying you have to, but give it some thought. In shaa Allah, you won't have to live like this forever."

Shaheer's mind buzzed. He imagined what it would be like to make friends he wouldn't have to leave behind.

To not be afraid of getting attached to a place because it always ended up in the rearview mirror as they drove away again. The longing squeezed his heart, but Shaheer knew his options: face disappointment or don't bother to care.

Shaheer didn't bother. He was over it.

2
ASHAR

Ashar crouched low over his hockey stick, skates digging into the ice like knives. Through his helmet's face cage, Ashar watched Sohaib peel across the rink, kicking up a plume of white powder as he charged forward with the puck.

Coach split them up into two teams of seven for practice. Having Sohaib on the "opposing" team made Ashar extra glad they were always on the same side in a real game. Sohaib was a force of nature. That was why he was their center.

But Ashar was a worthy defenseman and he wasn't about to let his teammate outplay him, even in a fake game.

Sohaib made a flawless pass to Daniel. Daniel threaded

away from the winger on Ashar's side, but the winger shot his stick up to block his opponent.

Coach Taylor blew his whistle in one sharp note. "Penalty! No hooking!"

C'mon, Jamal, Ashar thought. The Husky Bladers' best wing was, ironically, a penalty magnet.

Daniel resumed his trek across the ice. Ashar was ready for him. Heart pounding, he kicked off, intercepting Daniel at the blue line to block the pass headed back in Sohaib's direction. Ashar tried to get the puck away from his side's goal, but a biting pinch in his toes caused him to wince, sending his swing off-kilter. The puck skidded deeper into his own defensive zone instead of the other team's.

Ugh! *Are you kidding me?*

Sohaib's eyes bored into Ashar from behind his face shield like *What was that?* Color seeped into Ashar's cheeks. *That* had been a sloppy wrist. A rookie mistake. Embarrassment lanced Ashar's chest like hot steel, and without a second thought, he abandoned his post and veered to snatch the puck up before one of their opponents got to it first. Jamal made a noise of protest as Ashar cut him off, but Ashar didn't stop. He stole the puck with his hockey stick and turned back and sped across the center line toward the opposite goal, ignoring the cramping in his feet.

"What do you think you're doing?" Jamal called out to him.

But Ashar's ears were filled with cotton as he focused on reaching Ramiz, the Husky Bladers' formidable goalie. He took a shot, and Ramiz blocked it effortlessly.

"And that's time!" Coach Taylor bellowed. He clapped his hands, the sound echoing around the rink. "Good job, everyone."

"Good job, my foot!" Jamal said, skating up to Ashar and almost barreling him over. He was mad as a bull as he jabbed a finger in Ashar's shoulder. "You can't just take random swipes at the puck whenever you want! Stick to your own position instead of stealing someone else's and charging ahead without a plan, would you?"

"I had a plan! I just messed up!" Ashar protested. "Then I tried to fix it."

"It's not your job to fix it!"

"Break it up, boys," Coach Taylor said. He zeroed in on Ashar's face as Ashar stomped past him to grab his water bottle from the bench. Coach Taylor looked tougher than nails. He was six foot four, meaty armed, and bald, with a perpetually blotchy pink face. Total ex-military.

"Don't fret over that pass," Coach Taylor remarked. "Happens to the best players. But there's no point in going rogue." Coach's expression was always neutral, whether he was chiding or trying to comfort. Ashar was used to it, but right then, it embarrassed him even more. He couldn't afford to make beginner mistakes. Ashar hadn't been playing ice hockey long—only since fifth grade—while the rest of the guys probably learned to slide around on the ice in their diapers. His uncle always told him it was never too late to start doing what you love, but every blunder Ashar made was a reminder that he was technically behind, and if he didn't pull himself together, there was no way the Arlington Academy Icecaps were going to welcome him onto their team. If he even got into the school.

Arlington Academy of Science and Technology was the number one high school in the country, and it was supercompetitive to get into. Their ice hockey team was legendary. Arlington was at the tippy top of college recruitment lists on the East Coast. The more prestigious the team he was on, the better Ashar's chances were of making it to the big leagues, so becoming an Icecap was one gigantic leap closer to the NHL.

Ashar should feel lucky he was even on the Husky

Bladers. Coach said he liked his potential, which was a nice way of saying "good, but not good enough." Ashar didn't do *good enough*.

The others joined in a circle around Coach Taylor at the edge of the rink. Their parents had started arriving, watching them from the bleachers or talking among themselves. Ashar spotted Mom sitting on the middle bleacher, her dark head bent over the iPad in her lap. Probably finalizing lesson plans while she waited for her son's practice to be over.

"All right, guys. I'm loving the energy out there." This, of course, Coach said with as much emotion as a statue. "Keep that up and we might stand a chance this year against the Cardinals. Enjoy your day off tomorrow and I'll see you back here on Tuesday. We'll go over our plan of attack then. Good luck on your first day of school."

They all climbed out of the rink, patting one another on the back. Ashar could feel their excitement about the upcoming season.

"Hey, lighten up! You played great," Ramiz said to Ashar. He gave Ashar a fist bump that Ashar didn't feel like he deserved, but it was hard to say no to Ramiz. "See you at school!" Ramiz waved at Ashar and Eddie over his shoulder. The three of them attended Farmwell Station Middle School, while Jamal, Daniel, and Sohaib were in different districts. All of them were starting the eighth grade tomorrow.

Ashar took off his headgear, cold sweat dripping down his forehead and the front of his jersey. He felt so proud every time he pulled on the purple jersey with the number 29 and MALIK printed on the back.

"Hey, sweetie," Mom said as Ashar approached her. She helped him take off all the layers of padding on his shoulders, elbows, and knees, along with his mouth guard, neck guard, and gloves.

Ashar sat down next to her and slid his skates off miserably. His toes were starting to blister. "Did you see that?"

"See what?" asked Mom.

"How bad I sucked."

"You did not suck. You're always great out there," Mom said, mussing his hair. She looked tired, but everything about Mom—from her round doll face to her mane of wavy black hair ending just above her waist to her long-lashed brown eyes—screamed for attention. She looked like one of those actresses in the Pakistani dramas that Ashar's aunt was obsessed with. Even her name—Zareena—sounded like a princess's.

"You're just saying that because you have to," Ashar said.

"Fine. I've seen penguins play better than you. Happy?" She gave her son a tight smile. "Stop putting yourself down. Chalo. Zohra's family is coming over for dinner. I still have to put the lasagna in the oven."

Ashar carried his sports bag over one shoulder as they headed out of the skating rink. Coach Taylor nodded at them as they walked by, hands folded across his broad chest, but Ashar didn't miss the slight droop in his mouth, as if Ashar had done something to displease him.

◆ ◆ ◆

Ashar dropped his bag and equipment next to the front door of their new house. Well, it was a rental, but thinking of it as *theirs* made Ashar giddy. He forgot all about how bad practice had been.

Ashar and Mom had gotten the town house three weeks ago after living in Ayoub Mamou's—Mom's older brother—basement for years. Mom was a high school math teacher. She was always up-front with Ashar about money. If something wasn't possible, then it just wasn't. And for the longest time, having their own place had been out of the question. Her application had only been accepted because Ayoub Mamou put his name down on the lease, too. The house was much older and smaller than his uncle's, but Ashar didn't care. For the first time, they had a place to call their own.

"Namaz first," Mom instructed.

While Mom prepped for their guests in the kitchen, Ashar took a quick shower and made wudu in the upstairs bathroom before praying in his room. He made dua for the Husky Bladers to kick butt in every game and for him to get a grip (literally) on his passing. He also asked to get into Arlington Academy. Ashar had dreamed about going there since elementary school, when he met an older boy in his old Sunday school class who went to the academy and told Ashar all about how amazing it was. Ashar had been moon-eyed over going there ever since, especially when he learned about the Icecaps. He *had* to be part of their team. Mom was down for him going to Arlington, too, even though it was about an hour away. Luckily, there was a bus. But first, Ashar had to pass the grueling entrance exam in November. Arlington Academy was a STEM-heavy school, and Ashar's least favorite subject was science.

When Ashar was done praying, he hurried downstairs to help Mom, but skidded to a halt at the literal buffet spread out on the counter. "Whoa! I wasn't gone that long! What happened?"

"Oh," Mom said. "I had time while you were at practice, so I expanded tonight's menu a little."

A *little*? Ashar eyed the five different items apart from the lasagna and the bowl of chaat for appetizers. All for just five people. Ashar got an uneasy feeling in the pit of his stomach. On a regular day, Mom was a master chef. Everyone in the family called her the Queen of Twenty-Minute Meals. But Ashar knew she overcooked when she was stressed.

"Is everything okay?" he asked her.

Mom flinched like he'd caught her stealing. She looked even more tired than she had earlier. "Yeah, why do you ask?"

Busted. Her voice squeaked when she lied. But before Ashar could grill her, the doorbell rang, and Mom asked him to get it while she obsessively tidied the already clean kitchen.

"Yo, salam!" Ayoub Mamou greeted him when Ashar opened the door. While his uncle hugged him, his cousin Zohra slipped inside and started undoing her sandals without acknowledging Ashar. Zohra was only two months older than him. They'd grown up like brother and sister since they'd lived together for basically their whole lives. But lately, Zohra hadn't been acting like herself. She'd even stopped replying to Ashar's texts and his comments under her social media posts. Zohra liked to have the last word, so it was kind of bizarre.

"Where's bhabi?" Mom asked them in the kitchen.

"Faiza couldn't make it. She already had a friend thing planned," said Ayoub Mamou.

"What? Who's gonna eat all this food?" Mom gestured to the counter.

Ayoub Mamou and Zohra raised their hands and said "Me!" in unison.

"Fine. You better take all the leftovers home with you, too."

Zohra sat down at the table next to Ashar, but she kept her body angled away from him.

"Why are you mad at me?" Ashar whispered so that the grown-ups wouldn't hear. He'd asked before, with no luck, but he wasn't the type to give up.

Zohra brushed her pink-tipped hair out of her face. "It smells so good, Zareena Phuppo," she said like Ashar hadn't spoken. Ashar felt steam coming out of his ears.

"Have as much as you like. Don't be shy. This is your

home, too," Mom said. Zohra's mouth twitched slightly, but she helped herself.

"How was practice, Ash?" asked Ayoub Mamou. The pile of food in front of him reflected off his glasses. Ayoub Mamou was the reason why Ashar had gotten into ice hockey. He was a hard-core Capitals fan, and they used to go skating together. Their family never missed one of Ashar's games, or Zohra's band concerts, where she played flute.

"I kept lifting the puck and was told I'm too impulsive," Ashar said, stabbing at the lasagna with his fork.

Zohra fake gasped. "You? Impulsive? Get out of here."

Ayoub Mamou laughed out loud at that. "Sorry," he said, covering his mouth with a napkin. "What I meant is, don't let it get to you. How many times have we seen an NHL player screw up so bad we thought their career was over?"

"I guess," said Ashar. He would've been insulted had it been anyone else laughing at him, but he couldn't be annoyed at his uncle. He loved how carefree Ayoub Mamou was. Mom was more the down-to-business type, but Ayoub Mamou acted like everything was a joke, and he especially loved to pick on his little sister. It made

Ashar wish he had a sibling, especially right now, with how Zohra was treating him for no good reason.

Ayoub Mamou was the closest thing to a dad he'd ever had. Ashar's real dad was like smoke to him, barely visible. Like his reflection on the ice rink after dozens of skates mucked it up before the Zamboni smoothed over the surface. All Ashar knew was that Mom. Hated. His. Dad's. Guts. Ashar never truly missed having a dad because he had Ayoub Mamou. But still. He always wondered.

"Hey, Mom," Ashar said, "I forgot to tell you. Some of my gear is getting old. I need new stuff."

Mom lowered her spoon, eyebrows knitting together. "What needs to be replaced?"

"Well, for starters, my skates are getting kinda tight."

"Your *skates*?" Mom exclaimed.

"I'm no doctor, but I'm pretty sure feet grow as we age," said Ayoub Mamou. Mom shot him a look before turning back to Ashar.

"Do you need them right now?" she asked.

"I mean, my feet have started hurting. I don't want that to affect how I play." *Can't afford to look worse than I already do in front of Coach and the team*, Ashar thought. Practice might've been a dud today, but Ashar loved ice hockey. Just being on the ice, communicating with the other Husky Bladers in a language all their own—Ashar couldn't describe it. It felt right, and that made him want to give the sport his all.

"And you still want to do the Arlington test prep class?" Mom said.

"Yeah, of course," Ashar said, confused. What did that have to do with new skates?

Mom slumped back in her chair, and Ashar could tell by her expression that he wasn't going to like what came next.

"Ashar, I'm sorry. I can't pay for you to play ice hockey *and* prepare for the exam. I thought I could, but—unfortunately, with all the new bills, I can't afford it. That's the trade-off for having our own place."

Ashar snapped his head at her. His chest felt like it was going to combust. She was making him choose between getting into Arlington and playing for the Husky Bladers? The two things that were most important to him!

He knew they weren't rich by any means. Mom made just enough at her teaching job—sometimes tutoring on the side—for them to survive. Ashar was used to only getting the things he really wanted on special occasions, like on Eid or his birthday. But he wished just once he didn't have to give something up! Ashar looked at Ayoub Mamou to back him up.

"I could buy him the new skates—" Ayoub Mamou started, but Mom shut him down, saying that he'd helped them enough. "Oh, come on, Zareena," he said.

"Yeah, why can't he?" Ashar argued. "He's like my dad."

"Then you should move back in with us," Zohra said.

"Why? So you can ignore me there, too?" Ashar lashed out at her.

"What's wrong with our house?" Zohra shot back.

"Nothing! What's wrong with *you*?"

"Enough!" Mom said. "You don't *have* to go to Arlington. The schools in this county are good, too."

"But the schools in this county don't have the Icecaps!" Without a proper tutor, Ashar's chances of getting into Arlington were slim to none. Why did the best high school team have to be a bunch of geniuses, too?

"Listen, Ash. Your grades are fine, and you know I'll help you study for the math portion. But if you've made your choice to play ice hockey, then the rest is on you," said Mom.

"*Yeah*, I pick ice hockey," said Ashar. But that meant he was on his own in reading and science. He sucked at science. Earth science, life science, you name it. Memorizing facts was not Ashar's thing. Arlington disintegrated before Ashar's eyes. Ayoub Mamou lifted a shoulder at him apologetically. Even Zohra looked sorry for him.

And because he was *impulsive*, Ashar slapped his fork down, pushed out of his chair, ran upstairs, and slammed his door.

3
SHAHEER

The next morning, Shaheer quickly grabbed a banana and a granola bar from the kitchen and booked it before Dada nagged him about eating a real breakfast. Dad had already left for the hospital, so Shaheer put on his helmet and rode the short bike ride from the apartment to school without anyone to see him off.

He went straight to the main office and introduced himself to the friendly-looking secretary. Shaheer used the same line every time: *Hi, I'm new. Can I get my schedule? No, I don't need anyone to show me around. Just a map is fine.*

This time, however, the secretary gave him a strange look. "Haven't I seen you around before?" she asked.

"No. I just moved here," said Shaheer.

She appraised him for a beat too long but eventually printed out and handed his schedule to him. "All eighth graders report to the auditorium every morning before the bell. It's across the hall."

"Thanks." Shaheer put his AirPods in without taking the time to look at his surroundings. His brain was mostly logged off at school, awake just enough to pay attention if he was called on and go through the motions of doing assignments and turning in homework. He took a seat all the way in the back of the auditorium. It was still pretty empty because school didn't start for another thirty minutes. The only person near him was a brown-skinned hijabi girl a few chairs down. Her head was bent over a sketchbook, and it was like the rest of the world didn't exist as she worked. Shaheer wondered when she would notice the lead smearing her sleeve.

Looking away from the girl, Shaheer tore open his granola bar and took a bite as he taped his schedule to the front of a folder. As he reviewed it, he suddenly got the feeling that he was being watched, and looked up.

A girl two rows in front of him—he hadn't noticed her come in—was glaring at him through white glasses. Her eyes and pink-tipped braids were two shades darker than her brown skin. There was something about her expression that told Shaheer he shouldn't mess with her. He took one AirPod out of his ear as if to say, *Can I help you?*

The girl's eyebrows weaved in anger, and she showed him her back. A few seconds later, she turned around again with her arms crossed. "What on earth did you do to your *hair*?" she demanded. "Is that a wig?"

Shaheer looked over his shoulder, but there was only a wall. She was obviously talking to him. He gaped at her, speechless, then averted his gaze, pretending like he hadn't heard the rude comment.

"So you're just gonna ignore me now?" she spat.

Shaheer was very confused. "I don't even know you," he said.

The girl looked indignant, her cheeks bruising pink. She muttered "jerk" underneath her breath, grabbed the slender black instrument case at her feet, and moved to the other side of the auditorium. Shaheer could only watch, perplexed. *Wow, okay.* He put his earbud back in and turned up the volume, so he didn't hear when someone came up behind him this time and clapped him on the back so hard that his AirPods fell out of his ears.

"Hey, man. Found you. Whoa! That hairdo." A desi boy with curly hair in a Ronaldo jersey and a blond-haired white boy sandwiched Shaheer between them as they sat down with their backpacks. "What'd you use? MiracleGro?" The desi boy tugged at a strand of Shaheer's hair from the back. Shaheer slapped the stranger's hand away, probably harder than he'd intended to.

"Coach will lose it if it falls into your eyes. You'll need to wear a headband underneath your helmet," said the blond-haired boy. He smirked. "Or put it in a man bun!"

Shaheer swung his head back and forth at them. *Is this a dream? Am I even awake?*

"Anyway, I texted you and you didn't reply," said Ronaldo boy. "Get this. Evelyn Carr's parents—the ones who own the pizza shop—are giving away free treats after school. Everyone's going. You in? Ashar? Hello?" he prompted when Shaheer gawked at them.

"Look, I don't know who you guys think I am, but I'm not him," Shaheer finally got out. "My name's not Ashar."

The two boys stared at Shaheer for a split second, then laughed. "Very funny. Are you trying to prank us? Is that what this whole getup is about?" the blond asked.

"I swear you have the wrong guy," said Shaheer.

"Yeah, yeah. Whatever. Are you coming with us after school or not?"

Frustrated that they weren't listening and were still invading his space, Shaheer grabbed his bag and stood up. "Leave me alone," he hissed at them. He climbed over the chair in front of him and the one after that to put at least one row between himself and the two boys. Shaheer could feel their bewildered looks on his back. He heard them whisper things like "He okay?" and "Maybe he's still grumpy after yesterday" and "Think Zohra knows what's up?"

Shaheer kept his earbuds in and his music loud, blocking out all other sounds in the auditorium as eighth graders started to pile in. Right up until the bell rang, Shaheer couldn't shake the feeling that everyone was spying on him.

✦ ✦ ✦

Shaheer found his homeroom easily in House A, the section reserved for eighth-grade lockers and classes. He'd been desperate to escape the auditorium after that weird encounter, but the relief shriveled up when he walked into homeroom and spotted the girl with white glasses from earlier.

She clocked him right there. "What are you doing here? This is not your homeroom."

"Yes, it is," Shaheer said with forced calm. To prove it, he held up his folder with the taped schedule for her to read. Shaheer noticed her own schedule out on her desk, and he picked out her name at the top: Zohra Ayoub.

Zohra's eyes raked down and across the page. "'Shaheer Atique'?" she said. "But that's not—what's going on?"

"You tell me," Shaheer said. "The lady in the front office, you, those two other guys this morning. You're all mixing me up for this Ashar guy. I'm not him, okay?"

Zohra peered at him closely, eyebrows furrowed with an intense but genuinely puzzled look on her face. Eventually, she backed away from him like he'd sneezed on her and shot him odd looks all through morning announcements. Like she was trying to figure him out. Maybe to make sure he was real. Shaheer didn't know. All he knew was that Zohra wasn't the only one. He caught a couple of other people in his homeroom look away quickly when he caught them staring at him. Shaheer wanted to scream at them to stop.

Instead, he lay low and hightailed it to first block as soon as the bell set him free.

4
ASHAR

Ashar was *not* a morning person. If someone tried talking to him before he was wide awake, irritation invaded his whole body like a swarm of bees. Mom liked to be at work early, and now that they lived alone, she wouldn't let him take the bus because she didn't trust him not to miss it. So he had to get up and leave the house with her, which meant he got dropped off too early for it to be legal. Plus, he was still in a bad mood after last night. Mom tried to cheer him up by promising to buy him new skates ASAP, but it didn't help.

With his extra time, Ashar decided to skip the auditorium and go to the library to print out as many practice tests as he could get his hands on. Since he wasn't going to a formal prep class anymore, Ashar had to come up with his own strategy. He would take one practice test every week until the Arlington admission exam in November. He'd watch Khan Academy videos until his brain fizzled out. Not having a tutor wasn't going to stop him. He was *going* to get into Arlington and join the Icecaps.

When the bell rang, Ashar hoisted his now-heavy backpack and left the library to go to homeroom. A few students and teachers gave him drowsy first-day sort of waves in the hallway. His phone vibrated with a text after leaving homeroom for first block. It was from Zohra. He had a couple of other unread messages from Eddie and Ramiz, but he read hers first.

> **Zohra:** Where are you??
>
> **Ashar:** Going to 1st block. Lang arts with Burnes
>
> **Zohra:** Something weird is going on. There's this new kid that looks exactly like you. It's freaking everyone out

Guess Zohra forgot that she was supposed to be mad at him.

> **Ashar:** So you're saying he's cute?

Zohra: I'm not kidding, Ash!! We're all confused!

Ashar rolled his eyes at the screen. His cousin was overreacting. When he finally made it to his language arts class in House A, a handful of students were already there, and Mr. Burnes was digging for something through his desk drawers.

Ashar plopped his bag down on the nearest desk. He rubbed his eyes and yawned, feeling the sleep he'd lost. He was stressed out about how he was going to fit in studying for the Arlington exam on top of regular home-work and ice hockey. The reading section he might be able to pull off, but *science*?

Ashar opened his bag to fish for a pencil, thinking his only choice was to study before school, between classes, during lunch—

A shoulder rammed into Ashar, knocking his bag out of his hand and spilling its contents onto the floor. At any other moment, Ashar wouldn't have made a big deal out of it. But his tiredness, mixed with disappointment and worry, set him off.

"Would you watch where you're going?" Ashar snapped, bending down to pick up his things.

"Sorry. Didn't see you," said another boy's voice.

"Then next time don't walk around with your eyes clos—" Ashar raised his head, and his voice caught in his throat like someone had hit his off switch. A gasp caught in Ashar's throat and he jerked back like the boy in front of him was a hot plate that would burn him.

Those were *his* brown eyes that sat a little too far apart on his face. His button nose. His wavy black hair if he let it grow out. Oh God, he even had the same freckle on his upper lip.

The other boy—this other Ashar—looked equally astonished, his eyes bulging out of their sockets.

Ashar screamed first, startling everyone.

Mr. Burnes shot up to his full not-so-tall height. "Excuse me! Was that necessary?"

Ashar and other-Ashar stared at each other like their teacher hadn't said anything, the former half leaning against the desk, the latter frozen with both hands limp at his sides.

"Gentlemen," Mr. Burnes prodded. "One of you isn't supposed to be in here."

Not-Ashar blinked at the comment. "Why not?"

"Siblings aren't put in the same classes together."

"We're not brothers," the boys emphasized together.

Mr. Burnes pressed a button on his computer's keyboard. "Names?"

"Shaheer Atique."

Ashar's stomach roiled at the name. "Ashar Malik," he said, feeling woozy.

"So *you're* Ashar," said Shaheer. "People have been getting us mixed up all morning."

"Jeez, I wonder why!" Ashar exclaimed. Zohra *hadn't* been exaggerating. This kid was Ashar's literal doppelgänger! Besides the hair, the only difference between him and Shaheer was that Shaheer was a tad bit skinnier compared with Ashar's more athletic build.

"Interesting," Mr. Burnes interrupted, squinting at his computer screen. "You're both on my roster. Guidance doesn't usually make a mistake like that. Are you two *sure* you're not related?" he asked with more than a hint of skepticism. Ashar didn't blame him for not believing them. He'd think he was trippin' if he'd been in Mr. Burnes's shoes, too. But it was still an absurd question.

"What do you mean, are we *sure*?" asked Ashar. "Wouldn't we know that? I've never seen him before in my life," he added for good measure.

Shaheer didn't say a word. Ashar couldn't read his

face. If he was flipping out on the inside like Ashar was, he was doing a pretty good job of hiding it.

"He's telling the truth, Mr. Burnes," piped up Val Lopez. "We've all known Ashar since elementary school. Shaheer is new."

Mr. Burnes passed one last look over them and appeared to finally take their word for it. "All right, then. Have a seat."

Shaheer chose the desk next to Ashar. Ashar wished he hadn't. He didn't like looking at Shaheer too closely. It felt like bugs were crawling all over him when he did. But Ashar didn't want to make it obvious by moving to the other side of the room. So he sat down beside his clone with one thought racing through his head:

I should've stayed in bed.

5
SHAHEER

Ashar was a fidgety kid. It was distracting, but Shaheer couldn't help snooping out of the corner of his eye. Foot tapping. Pencil spinning. Face scratching. Shaheer's own knees were shaking from leftover shock. Everything that had happened this morning made sense now. That didn't mean what was *currently* happening did, though. Shaheer was just glad he wasn't the only one who seemed baffled. The other kids in class ogled him and Ashar while Mr. Burnes went over the syllabus.

Shaheer wasn't very superstitious, but for a brief moment, he seriously wondered if Ashar was a jinn. They could shape-shift, and the bad ones liked to play tricks on humans. What else could explain him meeting his whole twin? Which he and Ashar weren't, obviously. It wasn't possible. The Property Brothers popped into his mind, and Shaheer imagined him and Ashar posing in front of a fixer-upper wearing tool belts.

I'm losing it, Shaheer thought. Needing a diversion, he tapped on his phone screen underneath his desk and adjusted the volume lower on his AirPods. His hair hid them from plain sight, and as long as he appeared to be paying attention, no one would notice.

Unfortunately, someone saw him pull that little trick. Shaheer shouldn't have been surprised Ashar was watching his every move, despite pretending he wasn't.

"You can't use those in class," Ashar whispered to him.

Shaheer snorted. "Don't see why it bothers you."

"You'll get in trouble."

Shaheer gave Ashar a hard look. "You gonna snitch on me? What are you, five? 'Cuz you sure are acting like it."

An angry flush leaped up Ashar's cheeks. "At least my mom taught me how to do my hair. Do you even own a brush, Shaggy?"

Definitely five. "Yeah. I do. What I don't have is a mom," Shaheer quipped. Ashar's tongue snapped back in his mouth like a tape measure.

"Ashar," said Mr. Burnes, jabbing a finger in Shaheer's

direction. "Why don't you read the next paragraph for us?"

"I'm not Ashar," Shaheer said with a frown in his voice.

Mr. Burnes didn't look embarrassed by his mistake. "Shaheer. You read it, then."

Shaheer slid the paper toward himself, panicking. He hadn't been following along and had no idea where to start.

"'Talking out of turn in class will first result in a warning,'" Mr. Burnes read out loud. "'Each occurrence after that will result in the appropriate disciplinary action.'" He stared pointedly in Shaheer and Ashar's direction. "There's your first warning, boys. Not a good way to start the year."

Shaheer fought to contain his temper. If Ashar had minded his own business, he wouldn't have talked at all. Only half an hour into his first class, and Ashar Malik was ruining all his plans to fly under the radar.

Shaheer gave Ashar a dirty look, then ignored him for the rest of the block.

6
ASHAR

Ashar glimpsed Shaheer only one other time after language arts. He veered off course to avoid walking past Shaheer in the hallway after lunch, choosing to be late to civics instead. Naturally, people were nosy about it. Ashar would be curious, too, if another classmate suddenly showed up to eighth grade with a parallel-universe version of himself.

"Your evil twin is in my PE class," Eddie said, taking a bite of pizza. A horde of eighth graders had walked a few blocks from Farmwell to invade the shopping center after school and hit up the Carrs' restaurant. The owners were handing out free first-day-of-school slices to everyone, so the place was packed.

"Knock it off," Ashar chided. None of them knew the

guy, and Ashar felt bad about what he'd said to Shaheer that morning and how he'd gotten both of them in trouble. He really needed to get a handle on his tongue. After all, it wasn't *their* fault they happened to look freakishly alike. Still made as much sense as square wheels, but with everything else going on in his head, Ashar didn't want to dwell on it.

"I'm just saying. Wouldn't it be eerie if he liked ice hockey, too?" said Eddie.

"Aren't twins supposed to be, like, opposites?" Ramiz said, licking sauce off his fingers. "I bet Shaheer's more creative than Ash."

Ashar dropped his pizza on his disposable plate. Heat flushed through his body. "Guys. He and I are *not* twins. You would know if I had a brother. Heck, *I* would know that! Will you please shut up about it now? I'm sick of everything being Shaheer this and Shaheer that."

"We were just kidding. Jeez, what's with you?" Eddie asked.

"Yeah, you're even more strung up than usual," said Ramiz. He paused, a smile tugging at his mouth. "Shaheer seems more chill. You got all the angst."

"You suck." Ashar couldn't tell his friends about his insecurities on the ice or about his family's money problems. He didn't need Shaheer turned into one more thing on the list.

"Aww. You suck, too. We're getting McFlurries across the street. Wanna come?" asked Ramiz.

Ashar sighed. He'd used up his month's allowance. Plus, he needed to get home before Mom got back and freaked out about him not being there. "Can't. I gotta go or my mom will think I got kidnapped."

"Okay. See ya," Eddie said, and he and Ramiz crossed the parking lot. Ashar had left the pizza parlor and started to walk in the direction of his house when he heard raised voices coming from the end of the sidewalk.

"I just wanna talk!" came a familiar voice.

"Get out of my way!"

Oh no. What now? Ashar turned the corner of the Dunkin' at the end of the building and saw Zohra jump in front of a bicycle. Shaheer had to pump his brakes to avoid hitting her. "Move," he pleaded at her.

"Oh, come on! I didn't mean to bully you this morning. I thought you were Ashar."

"Zohra," Ashar said. "What's going on?"

Zohra spun around at his voice. Shaheer gave Ashar a flat look over her shoulder.

"Oh, hey," Zohra said. She stayed planted in front of Shaheer's bike with her hands on her hips.

"Your girlfriend's being a bully," Shaheer accused him.

Ashar made a face. "She's my cousin. Zo, why are you bugging him?"

Zohra flashed him an annoyed look and turned back to Shaheer. "I wanna make it up to you. I'll buy you a doughnut."

"No, thanks. I said it was *fine*," Shaheer said.

Why was Zohra insisting so hard? There was a glint behind her glasses he couldn't read.

Zohra stepped forward, putting her hands on the handlebar. *"Please?"*

Shaheer exhaled loudly. "If I say yes, will you leave me alone forever?"

"Deal. You're coming, too." Zohra yanked Ashar by his shirt collar into the cool of the Dunkin's AC.

Ashar wiggled out of her grip. "What are you doing?" he said through clenched teeth. Ashar looked nervously at Shaheer, who was leaning his bike against the wall. They hadn't gotten off on the right foot, and he didn't think doughnuts were going to make up for holding him hostage.

"Play along" was all Zohra told him. She ordered

Shaheer a Boston Kreme and a strawberry-frosted dough-nut for herself.

"Aren't you getting one?" Shaheer asked to Ashar's surprise.

Ashar glanced at his favorite maple-syrup doughnut on the rack and looked away quickly. "I'm good."

Shaheer eyed him, then pointed at the display. "Can we get one of those, too?" he asked the cashier.

Ashar's face burned. "No. It's okay. I'm not hungry."

"Sure, you're not." Another protest rose in Ashar's throat, but Shaheer was already handing a sleek black credit card over the counter, waving off the cash Zohra was trying to hand the cashier. *Whoa, fancy.* That explained Shaheer's bike, his nice clothes, and his swanky shoes. He even had the latest phone.

"Wow, thanks." Zohra whistled. "Your parents gave you that? Mine would never."

Shaheer shrugged. "I only use it when I have to. My dad's an ER doctor so he's not around a lot."

"Cool!" Zohra said as they sat down at a table. "I bet he's got tons of stories."

Shaheer blinked, as if he'd never considered that before. "I don't know. We're not close."

Zohra casually took a bite of her doughnut. "What about your mom?"

Terror seized Ashar. He tried to send Zohra a telepathic signal. *Abort! Abort!*

"My parents are divorced," Shaheer replied coolly. "My dad moves us around a lot."

"Where else have you lived?" Ashar asked, curiosity getting the better of him.

"Mostly big cities. We were in Boston last."

"So you've been all over the place, huh?" Zohra cupped her face in her hands and leveled her eyes at Shaheer. "The only other place we go to is New Jersey to visit distant family. Right, Ashar?" She bumped Ashar with her elbow. Last night, she would've gladly stabbed him with a fork.

Ashar nodded, trying to follow where Zohra was going with this.

"I was born in New Jersey," Shaheer said.

Ashar's heart thumped, a creeping feeling tapping at his brain. Like when you hear a story as a little kid, and again when you're older. The details are fuzzy, but you know you've heard it somewhere.

The wheels were turning so fast in Zohra's head, Ashar

thought they'd fly out of her ears. "Shaheer, when's your birthday?"

It finally hit Ashar what Zohra was getting at. He had the sudden urge to stop it, like watching a horror movie and knowing that a very bad thing was waiting behind the creepy door. Ashar knew like he knew the monster was behind it what Shaheer was gonna say.

Please don't say—

"April eleventh. Why?"

Triumph flickered across Zohra's expression. "What a coincidence. So is Ashar's."

Shaheer paused with his doughnut in front of his mouth. "That's . . . weird."

"Especially since you guys look alike," Zohra added.

Ashar wanted to scream at her to stop talking, but his lips felt like they were sewn together.

Shaheer groaned. "Not that much. I think everyone's exaggerating. Besides, I look like my dad."

Ashar's mouth opened, then closed. He concentrated on a spot on the floor before lifting his gaze back up to Shaheer with no humor.

"I don't know much about my dad. I wasn't even a year old when he and Mom separated. Don't have pictures either. When you said you look like your dad, I thought, well, I look kinda different from my mom, and"—Ashar knew he was rambling, but he kept going—"I don't know why I'm telling you this. Lots of people get divorced. It doesn't mean anything."

Shaheer was silent and, for once, so was Zohra. "What do you know about your dad?" Shaheer asked Ashar.

Ashar lifted one shoulder, a sad look crossing his face. "Not a lot. Mom hates talking about him. Literally the only thing I know is his first name."

Shaheer swallowed before asking another question. "What's his name?"

"Jawad."

Shaheer went rigid. "That's *my* dad's name," he said softly.

Ashar gaped at him, his throat threatening to close up again. "Do you know what your mom's name is?"

"Zareena."

Ashar gasped, covering his mouth, and he knew. *They* knew.

Neither of them had realized they'd gotten to their feet and were standing right in front of each other. Ashar breathed heavily, heat prickling down his spine.

"Are we—?"

"We can't be—"

They jolted back from each other as if tugged by an invisible force and landed on the floor, drawing attention from the employees behind the counter.

"Yeah." Zohra stuffed the rest of her doughnut in her mouth and waved a hand like the scene in front of her was no big deal. "You're twins. Called it."

7
SHAHEER

Shaheer's ears wouldn't stop ringing. *Twins.*

A small tornado ripped through Shaheer's head, uprooting everything he thought he knew. All kinds of words bubbled up in his mouth, but as usual, nothing came out. Shaheer's heart was beating so hard he thought it might jump right out of his chest.

Get involved. Make friends, Dad had said. *It'll be fun*, he said.

Shaheer was *not* having fun.

"This can't be real," Ashar breathed, shaking his head. His eyes swirled with emotions. "Why wouldn't Mom tell me I had a brother this whole time? No, there's gotta be a mistake. You're not in any of my baby pictures!"

Zohra turned to Ashar. "I heard my parents talking

one night. A few years ago. I swear I heard Papa say 'Ashar's brother' at one point, but I was half-asleep, so I thought my brain made it up. Then at school today, I thought, *what if?* What if what I heard was true? And here we are."

"But why would they lie to us?" Ashar exclaimed. He'd crawled back to the table and was hanging on to his chair like it was a life raft.

"It's not like we went up to them and asked, 'Hey, do I have a twin brother?' and they said, 'No.' They just didn't tell us," Shaheer said.

Zohra rolled her eyes. "Typical desi parents."

Shaheer crossed his arms. "Besides, we could be freaking out over nothing. Maybe there's a good explanation for all this."

"Like what?" asked Zohra.

Shaheer mined for one. *Grasping for straws*, Dada would call it. "How do I know the two of you aren't messing with me? Ashar could be lying about when his birthday is."

"I am not! And what about our parents' names? How would I find that out?" Ashar said. *"Look at us!* I would never lie about something like this!"

The look on Ashar's face made Shaheer think he was

being honest. Ashar would have to be a good actor to pull this kind of thing off. From what Shaheer had seen of the other boy so far, he was no good at hiding how he felt.

This kid . . . was his brother. If that was true, then Dad and Dada had known this whole time. They'd never told him. Never even hinted at it. Anger suddenly boiled up inside Shaheer. Even *Dada*. The fact that he'd never told Shaheer, even in secret . . . yeah, big ouch. Had his grandfather been against his parents separating him and Ashar? If he wanted answers, Dada was the best source to go to. But Shaheer wasn't sure if telling him about Ashar was a good idea.

Well, he'd gone and found the long-lost twin brother they'd both tried to hide from him. Served them right.

The three of them sat wordlessly, doughnut crumbs littering the table in front of them. Shaheer's stomach lurched. His mind tuned out everything except for Ashar's presence. The room felt small, and the truth squatted like a monster between them, ready to lunge from the dark at any second.

"Did you ever try to look for your m—for Mom?" Ashar asked, breaking the silence.

"No. If she cared about me, she wouldn't have left," Shaheer said thinly. "Maybe she liked you better and that's why she kept you and gave me to Dad."

"Then that means Dad liked *you* better," said Ashar. "I tried looking for Dad. Searched everywhere online, but Jawad's a common Pakistani name. It didn't help." Ashar felt Zohra's eyes on the side of his face. He'd never told her that before. "I wonder what happened between them."

"Things ended badly."

"No kidding, Sherlock," said Zohra. "It's one thing for your parents to get divorced, but separating you guys, too? That's messed up."

Shaheer sighed. The conversation was draining the rest of his energy. "Listen, I don't want to talk about this anymore. I'm going home."

"How can you want to go home at a time like this?" Ashar said, sitting up. "Why are you acting like this is no big deal? Hey!"

Shaheer bounded out the door to his bike and Ashar and Zohra went after him.

"Shaheer, stop!" said Ashar.

"What do you want me to say?" Shaheer demanded. "I'm confused, okay?"

"All right. Say you go home. Then what? We're just gonna pretend like none of this ever happened?"

"Dude, I don't know!" Shaheer said, pulling at his hair. "Why are you asking so many questions?"

"Why aren't you?"

Shaheer took a deep breath. "If our parents didn't want us to know before, then they probably don't want us to know now. What's the point in telling them we found out?"

"Hundreds of points! Like the fact that I have a twin. That you have a brother and a cousin."

Shaheer's head spun. He looked at Zohra in a whole new light, and his hurt grew twofold. Yet another close family member whose existence had been kept from him.

"It's not *right*." Ashar started pacing the sidewalk. His nervous energy was infecting the air. "Why would they do this? What's the story?"

"Beats us. We found out the same time you did," Zohra said.

"So, let's ask them," Ashar suggested.

Shaheer leaned his forearms on his bike's handlebars and shook his head. "Dad won't talk. He'll come up with some random excuse to get out of the conversation and act like nothing happened." Or worse, he *wouldn't* ignore it and next thing Shaheer knew, Dad would be hauling them away again in a drastic attempt to keep him from Ashar. If Mom's name was banned under their roof, who's to say Ashar's wouldn't be, too?

Shaheer lifted his head, a sudden realization slamming into him. Dada's snide remarks to Dad for no reason, Dad getting all defensive. What if there *had* been a reason all along? That Dada was holding a grudge against Dad for letting Ashar go? There was already a chip on their shoulders. How much worse would it be if they found out Shaheer had discovered their secret?

"Seriously? Mom would blow her top. She hates talking about Dad. One time, I bugged her about him so much that she got mad and told me he was a—" Ashar silently mouthed a bad word.

Shaheer flinched. "Hey, he's not *that* bad."

"I'm just telling you what she said."

"Cool, so they hate each other. Nothing we can do. Good talk." Shaheer tried escaping again. Ashar grabbed hold of his shoulder to start to protest, but Zohra cut him off.

"Leave him alone, Ashar," she berated him. "Not everyone's gung-ho to learn about a secret sibling. It's okay, Shaheer," she added more softly. "It's a lot to process. Take your time. Catch you tomorrow?"

Yeah, we'll see about that, Shaheer thought as he shook Ashar off and pedaled away without looking back. He might pull the too-sick-to-go-to-school and stay-in-bed-like-a-blanket-burrito card early this year.

8
ASHAR

"I can't believe you just let him go like that!" Ashar complained.

"What were we supposed to do?" Zohra asked, hands splayed at her sides. "Tie him up? Give him time. He'll come around. Besides, at least *one* of you is reacting like a normal person to such major news."

Okay, it hadn't been more than fifteen minutes since everything he thought he knew about his family had been upended, and Zohra's attitude wasn't helping. What was *with* her? They'd fought plenty growing up, but this was on some other level.

"If that's what you think, then why are you here?" Ashar retorted. "You didn't have to go around playing detective. Go home. You can't stand to be around me any-more anyway."

Zohra shook her fists at him. "You are so *clueless*, Ash! Fine, I'll stay out of it. I'll leave you alone if that's what you want." She turned sharply and started walking away from him.

"Don't tell Ayoub Mamou anything about what hap-pened!" Ashar yelled after her. "He'll rat us out to Mom."

"Unlike somebody, I don't have a big mouth," Zohra said from the end of the sidewalk. "Where are you going? You don't live that way!"

"I'm going to find Eddie and Ramiz!" Except he wasn't. Ashar quickly checked the time on his phone before dashing across the street in the direction Shaheer had ridden off. The first day of school was always a little hectic for teachers, and Mom liked to have all her ducks in a row before wrapping up. There was enough time for Ashar to catch up to Shaheer before he needed to report back home. Zohra was welcome to sit around and wait, but Ashar wasn't going to do nothing when he'd just found his own *twin*. All he wanted was to talk to Shaheer. Maybe Shaheer would soften up if Ashar was there to help shoulder some of the blow. That's what brothers did, right?

Ashar ran as fast as his legs could carry him. He played one of the most strenuous and tiring sports. Sprinting a couple of miles didn't faze him, especially when he saw Shaheer way up ahead and pushed himself to run even faster. Shaheer was still too far away to hear Ashar if he shouted his name, though, and Ashar cursed underneath his breath when Shaheer rounded a bend and disappeared between the folds of an apartment complex.

Ashar stopped in front of the sign welcoming visitors to the community, spent. His feet ached in his worn sneakers. *Where did he go?* There were more than a dozen of the same-looking white buildings and he didn't know which one Shaheer lived in. Should Ashar search all of them until he found his bike parked outside?

"Shaheer?"

Ashar yelped at the unfamiliar voice. An old South Asian man in a T-shirt and track pants stood behind him on the pavement. "I thought I just saw you on your bike heading home," the old man said. "Or maybe not. Eyesight's not what it used to be. Did you get a haircut?" He was speaking Urdu, and Ashar silently thanked God that Mom had taught him the language. But the question made him sweat bullets like he was in full hockey gear. This man obviously thought *he* was Shaheer.

Was this—? No, this man couldn't be his dad. He was too old. Who was he, then?

The man stood there, and Ashar realized he was waiting for him to speak. "Yeah," Ashar blurted. "Haircut. It was getting long. Too much shampoo." *Too much shampoo? Really, Ashar?*

"Oh. I thought you liked that it was growing out. Anyway, I'm just finishing up my walk. I'm gonna go for one last round and meet you upstairs." And the old man gave Ashar the greatest gift ever by nodding toward a building nestled right up against the woods surrounding the neighborhood.

"Great, see ya there!" And Ashar bolted before he dug himself an even deeper hole. He needed to reach Shaheer before the old man did. *Shaheer's not gonna like this*, Ashar thought as he took the stairs up two at a time. So much for a brotherly chat.

On the second floor, Ashar spotted Shaheer's bike secured next to a green door marked 202. Panting, Ashar hammered on the door, his panic escalating with every second that it didn't open. Finally, it did, and Shaheer poked his head out in annoyance that immediately shifted to shock when he saw Ashar.

"What are *you* doing here?" Shaheer asked incredulously. "How did you find out where I live?"

"No time!" Ashar squirmed his way inside the apartment after checking that the coast was clear, despite Shaheer's objections. The last mad dash had stolen the rest of Ashar's breath, and he could only expel two words at a time. "Old man. Saw me. Thought I. Was you. He's coming!"

"I have no idea what you're—wait, old man?" Shaheer's eyes widened like saucers. "Dada saw you?"

Ashar blinked, his mind processing this new information. "We have a dada?" he yipped. "I can't believe this! A brother and a grandfather, and this whole time I didn't— it doesn't matter! He's already seen me and thinks you cut your hair!"

Shaheer's back smacked the coat closet like he couldn't stand upright anymore. "What were you *thinking*? Dada can't see us together! I don't know what his part was in the divorce and the whole splitting-us-up thing!" Ashar sensed it pained Shaheer to admit this. "If he snitches on us to Dad, there's no telling what he'll do! He might make me switch schools or pack us up and move again! I'm sick of it. Fix this!"

Ashar's heart sank. They couldn't move! Not before they even had a chance to figure out what had happened between Mom and Dad! Ashar instantly felt bad for jumping the gun and creating this mess, and for being the reason why Shaheer looked near hysterics. Then the word *switch* made a light bulb go off in his head.

"Switch places with me," Ashar said. "I'll stay here and pretend to be you while you go get a haircut. There's a barbershop next to the Dunkin' we were at earlier."

"You can't be me," Shaheer argued. "You don't know how!"

"What other choice do we have? Either suck it up or wait right here for Dada to get back and find us. Do you want to be at that surprise party? 'Cuz I don't."

"This cannot be happening," Shaheer grumbled.

Ashar bent down, picked up Shaheer's shoes, and thrust them into his hands along with his backpack before spinning him around and ushering him outside. "Go! Hurry. Leave your bike."

"I will not forgive you for this!" was the last thing Shaheer said before Ashar slammed the door in his face. In the wake of all the chaos, the sudden lull amplified how rapidly Ashar's heart was beating in his chest and narrowed his concentration down to his next problem: How do you impersonate someone you barely knew?

Ashar faced the apartment. If Shaheer hadn't answered the door, he would've thought he was in the wrong place. Save for one sofa, an armchair, a TV, and a breakfast table, the place stood virtually empty. Bland. Ashar wiped his sweaty palms on his jeans and slowly crept forward, taking in the apartment's layout like the walls would come to life and tell him exactly how to imitate Shaheer. When he heard the soft clicking sound of a doorknob, Ashar threw himself on the couch and scrambled for his phone. Then he quickly stashed it out of sight, fearing that it would prompt questions if his protective case was different from Shaheer's, but not before his shaky fingers dropped it on the carpet first.

Dada entered and lowered himself down on the sofa at Ashar's feet. "I found a beautiful trail just outside the neighborhood. It goes around a lake. We should go together one day. You can bring your bike."

"Sure," Ashar answered automatically, even though anxiety was shredding his insides to pulp over being in a strange place, talking to a stranger who was supposedly his grandfather while pretending to be his secret twin brother so they wouldn't get found out.

Dada stared at him as if he could read his mind. "I've never seen you wear those clothes, or those shoes by the door. Where'd you get them?"

"Found them buried somewhere," Ashar mumbled as another surge of terror seized him. *Please don't ask me any more questions.*

"You didn't wake me up this morning," Dada said. "What did you eat for breakfast? And did you have lunch?"

"I had a snack with some kids after school," Ashar said in a non-answer.

Dada looked like Ashar had smacked him. "You went out? With other kids? That . . . that's great! Who were they?"

Only the twin brother and cousin you and Dad "forgot" to tell him existed. Ashar shrugged and nestled deeper into the sofa. "Just some kids in my grade."

"Well, that's wonderful. Jawad'll be thrilled to hear it." Hearing Dad's name out loud was like a punch to the gut. It made the situation Ashar was in feel less like a bizarre role-playing game and more . . . real. Too real. His chest tightened.

Okay, enough fun for one day. He'd crawl out the window and risk breaking a couple of bones if that's what it took to escape, with or without meeting Dad. The longer he stuck around, the greater the chances that he would blow his cover, and it wasn't worth it if Shaheer was convinced Dad would do everything in his power to keep him away from Ashar.

"Where are you going?" Dada questioned Ashar when he stood up.

"Gonna take my bike out for a spin before starting on homework," Ashar said.

He breathed a sigh of relief when Dada nodded like that was perfectly normal. "Okay. I'm gonna take a quick nap. Wake me when you get back."

Ashar nodded, then zoomed out of there as casually as was humanly possible.

9
SHAHEER

Get a haircut. Ashar might as well have told Shaheer to fight a gorilla. The nerve of that other boy's two brain cells to follow him home, stir up trouble, and kick him out while ordering him around boiled Shaheer's blood. He should've thrown Ashar under the bus and let him clean up his own mess. That would teach him a lesson.

But whether Shaheer liked it or not, he and Ashar were in the same boat. If one of them sank, so did the other. And even though Ashar Malik had been a pain in the neck since that morning, Shaheer was curious enough about their past to not want to risk losing the opportunity to find out first.

But why did it have to be *this* way?

The stylist made a snipping motion at the ends of

Shaheer's locks. "How do you want it?" she asked, spraying Shaheer's head with enough water to sap a pool.

Shaheer was pawing at his head miserably when the little bell above the shop's door rang and in walked Ashar. His hair was standing up and his cheeks were all red from the wind.

A muscle twitched in Shaheer's cheek. "Ask *him*," he hissed.

Ashar came to stand beside Shaheer. "Ask me what?" he asked, sounding a little breathless.

"How does he want it to look?" the stylist repeated, running her hands through Shaheer's wet hair.

"Just like mine," Ashar said.

"Good choice. Suits both of your face shapes."

"Why can't I just wear a hat?" Shaheer mumbled.

"All the time?" Ashar rolled his eyes. "It's just hair, Shaheer. It'll grow back."

Shaheer wanted to snap at him that he wouldn't have to do this in the first place if Ashar hadn't royally goofed up, but figured it wasn't worth it.

Ashar sucked on a lollipop while Shaheer whispered goodbye to his hair. He kept his eyes tightly shut the way someone scared of heights would on a roller coaster. The scissor noises made him vaguely ill. He felt outright faint when feathery locks freely tumbled down his neck and the sides of his face. When the stylist finished up, brushing off stray hair and combing it to perfection, Ashar gasped. Shaheer took a deep breath and forced himself to look in the mirror. His jaw dropped. It was the shortest it'd been in a long time. If he and Ashar looked alike before, they were almost indistinguishable now.

"This is so *freaky*," Shaheer said, shuddering.

"You look fresh!" said the hairdresser.

Ashar put his face next to Shaheer's to look at their reflections together. He gave Shaheer an open smile that Shaheer imagined everybody ate up.

"You have to admit that's pretty cool," said Ashar.

Shaheer's nostrils flared. He yanked the styling cape off and paid at the front desk before marching outside. Ashar followed like a pesky shadow.

"I hope you're happy!" Shaheer fumed, pointing at his head.

"You're seriously this worked up over a haircut?" asked Ashar, crossing his arms.

"It's not just about the haircut! You nearly outed us! Who knows what could've happened if Dada found out we met? I don't know whose side he's on. What if he's still suspicious when I get back and starts interrogating me?"

"Chill, that won't happen. But listen. This whole impromptu swapping places thing gave me an idea. We want to know what happened that made Mom and Dad's divorce end up with them separating us, too, right? Maybe there's a way we can get them to talk," Ashar said. He clasped Shaheer's shoulders excitedly. The mischievous glint in Ashar's brown eyes immediately set off all Shaheer's alarms. Ashar grinned. "What if we switch places for real?"

Shaheer didn't respond for a long time. Finally, he pried Ashar's hands off his shoulders and said, "You're joking. What is switching places gonna do?"

"Think about it. Dad knows you," Ashar said. "And Mom knows me. Maybe if they get to know the other twin, too, they'll open up about what really happened."

Shaheer groaned. "Except we've already established that we've both tried before and neither of them would budge. What difference would it make if I pretend to be you or the other way around and tried doing the exact same thing?"

"We'll get them to accidentally bond with the other son by spending time with him! Then when we finally tell them the truth, they won't want to leave either of us behind again. They'll have to work things out if they want to continue seeing both of us. But we'll have to keep it a secret until the time is right, otherwise the connection won't stick. Easy! It's not like we're trying to get them married again," said Ashar.

Shaheer scoffed. "That's a horrible idea. Do you really think we'd be able to trick them?"

Ashar furrowed his eyebrows. "We're identical twins!" Ashar clearly thought his idea was brilliant and couldn't understand why Shaheer wasn't immediately on board.

"It doesn't matter. We're so different."

"They're not gonna find out. We can totally pull this off. I'll teach you to be me, and you teach me to be you. Come on, Shaheer. Aren't you dying to meet Mom?"

Shaheer hesitated. *Did* he want to meet his mom? She'd picked Ashar over him! If Shaheer wanted to find out why, now was his chance. They were in control here.

But the idea was still too risky. Shaheer knew better than to get attached to people or places. What if Ashar was being too optimistic and the plan didn't work? Mom and Dad had had the last thirteen years to prove that they cared about their other son, and neither of them came through. Why bother when it was clear to Shaheer that his own mom didn't want him?

Shaheer was too overwhelmed to decide right then

and there. "I don't know. I'll think about it. And will you give me space for *real* this time?"

Ashar gave a mock salute. "Yessir. Oh, and one more thing."

"What?" Shaheer said, taking up his bike.

"If Dada isn't awake when you get back, you might want to change into your pj's."

10
ASHAR

Mom texted Ashar instructions to take ingredients out so that dinner would be ready quicker when she got back from her long first day. Ashar was so distracted he opened and closed the fridge three times before noticing the marinating fish sitting on the top shelf right in front of his face. His mind was still ping-ponging when the front door opened, so he didn't register Mom's "Salam, I'm home!" at first.

Ashar flinched like she'd zapped him, and his hand knocked the entire cling-wrapped tray off the counter with a loud *crash*!

"Oh!" Mom dropped her bags in the den and rushed over to pick up the tray. "I wrapped these tightly so they're a little messy, but safe. Fish tacos are still on for dinner."

Ashar pretended to examine the fish with a whole lot of interest while Mom tied her long hair back with a claw clip.

"So how was your first day?" Mom asked in a singsong voice. She dove right into the kitchen to wash her hands and put the frying pan on the stove.

HMM, where do I start? Ashar thought, restraining himself from blowing up on her right there. The sting of betrayal was still fresh.

Mom turned to him from the pantry when she was met with silence. "Okay. Why are you so quiet? What's going on?" she asked, gathering supplies to whip up the sauce.

"Nothing," Ashar grunted, not trusting himself to say another word. He could already taste blood where he was biting down on his lower lip.

Mom looked at Ashar, who averted his gaze and went over to sit on the sofa to sort through his loud thoughts. He wanted to confront Mom. To wring the truth from her. But he had to hold it in until he talked to Shaheer tomorrow. This was about both of them.

"Hey, Ash," Mom said lightly. Too nicely. "If you want, we can start practicing on the math section tonight." Oh. She thought he was still upset about the pick-ice-hockey-or-Arlington thing. Strangely, the entrance exam had become a small blip in his brain. Guess accidentally finding out that you had a twin was a big deal or something.

"Sure," Ashar replied tightly.

"And we can stop by the icehouse later to buy your new skates."

"Yeah. Okay."

Mom's hand stilled on the mixing spoon. Her expression was sad, but it only twisted the frustration in Ashar's chest. She had no right! She was the one who'd kept Shaheer from him all this time! Not talking about his dad was one thing. At least he knew Dad existed in the first place. But to keep the secret about his own *brother* from him was another story.

What the heck had their parents been thinking? Did they really think Ashar and Shaheer would never find out? Did they *ever* plan on telling them? From what Zohra had said, it sounded like the rest of the family knew. Ayoub Mamou, Faiza Mami. They had all lied to him. The more he thought about it, the more it crushed his heart. Ashar took a deep breath to fend off the sob building in his chest.

"Ashar," Mom said. "You know I feel bad about the tutoring situation, right? For what it's worth, I make lots of dua for you. If you take the time to really hone down the science portion, I think you'll do fine on the exam."

"It's fine. Good thing I wanna play hockey. Would've sucked if I wanted to become, say, a *doctor*." Wow. Five minutes. A personal record.

Mom tensed. "Becoming a doctor is tough, anyway. It's a challenging career path."

"But so many desi parents want their kids to become doctors. How come you never want me to?" Ashar asked. He squinted at Mom from his seat on the couch, channeling his inner Detective Zohra to gauge her reaction.

Mom's eyebrows pinched together. "I never said you couldn't. Besides, don't you hate science?"

"I could learn to like it." Ashar could tell he was really starting to hit a nerve because Mom's hand clenched the counter. He searched her face for some kind of sign. *Do you miss him?* Ashar wondered. *Don't you love Shaheer, too?*

"You have plenty of time to think about the future," Mom said, abruptly ending the conversation. "Why don't you come put your tacos together while I fry?"

The opening beckoned and Ashar grabbed on before it slipped through his fingers.

"Wasn't Dad a doctor?"

Mom whipped around so fast her clip fell out of her

hair. Ashar's stomach churned like he'd swallowed an entire bottle of Halal Guys red sauce. Mom was giving him the same dark look as she had that one time he'd been called to the principal's office in kindergarten for stealing school supplies out of his classmates' desks.

I'm a dead man.

A note of authority crept into Mom's voice and teetered right on the edge of her teacher voice. "Who told you that?"

The fish was burning on the stove now, but she wasn't paying attention to it. Ashar held his breath. He couldn't tell her it had been Shaheer. How was he gonna explain this one?

"You might've brought it up once. I don't know . . ." Ashar trailed off, wilting under Mom's livid gaze.

She scowled and turned around to slap the air where smoke was curling up from the frying pan. "What a waste," she grumbled.

"How come I've never met him?" Ashar asked. "My dad."

"If he cared about you, he would have made the effort on his own," Mom said bluntly.

"What was the reason?" Ashar pushed. "The last straw for you guys?"

"Ashar," Mom said, her tone clipped. "You know I hate this topic. Please, I already have a lot on my plate."

"I just want to know!" The words burst from Ashar's mouth. He knew he was pushing Mom's buttons, but he didn't care. Not after today. "You can't keep it a secret forever!"

Ashar thought he was really going to get it now, but Mom surprised him by shutting the stove off and facing him stonily.

"We were married young, and I got pregnant while we were both settling into our jobs. Demanding careers with long hours and little time for each other. But we both wanted kids. We should have thought it through better instead of thinking it would fix our problems. It only got worse. We tried to work things out. We explored every avenue. In the end, it just wasn't meant to be. There. Now it's all out in the open. Happy?"

"Did you and Dad fight over who would keep me?"

Mom hesitated, and for a second, Ashar thought he could see the truth in her eyes. He wished she would stop the act and just admit he was a twin already. "It was a hard choice, but we both got what we wanted," she finally said. "Discussion over. Come eat."

Ashar sank deeper into the sofa so that only his eyes

peeped out over the top. Dad had always been a sore subject with Mom, but this was different. Mom never talked to him like that. There was something wrong with her. She was too irritable, too easily stressed all the time now.

Since the move. Since money became tight.

Ashar groaned. Talk about the worst time to introduce Shaheer to Mom. If only he and his brother had met sooner, when they were still living with Ayoub Mamou. He didn't want Shaheer to think Mom was a bad person, to see this side of her that even Ashar had never seen before. What if Mom took her frustration out on him during a switch and Shaheer decided he didn't want anything to do with her?

Maybe the whole trading places thing *was* a bad idea.

No. He'd already made up his mind. He needed to find out what happened that made his parents keep him from his brother. He didn't buy that Mom had let go of her other son so easily. That she *wanted* to. That didn't sound like the woman Ashar knew, the woman who raised him. Mom was religious, and she'd taught Ashar the importance of faith and family above all else. What made Shaheer any different from him? Mom never thought of him on his and Ashar's birthday? Didn't even care enough to send Shaheer a card or check in? She'd spent years pretending like Shaheer didn't even *exist*.

Ashar thought of all the first days of school he and Shaheer should've had together. All the birthday parties, the Eids, the pictures of ugly haircuts side by side they'd never have now, and something pinched Ashar between the ribs.

He wasn't going to back down. Ashar would meet Dad. He just hoped Shaheer felt the same way about Mom.

11
SHAHEER

Shaheer was stress-watching *Property Brothers* when Dad came home after the sun was already down.

"Hey, sport," he said cheerfully at seeing Shaheer in the living room. "Nice haircut. When did you decide to do that?"

Shaheer could only muster a shrug. "Today. Randomly," he said, trying to cut the chitchat before Dad asked about his day. He was *not* about to sit through that conversation. Shaheer's eyes stayed glued to the TV screen. Jonathan's crew was telling him that the fixer-upper's roof was leaking and the whole thing would have to be replaced. That's kind of how Shaheer felt, like every *drip drip drip* of his thoughts was going to collapse his insides.

Dad startled at the sight of the kitchen, where a greasy

mess splattered the stove and sink. "What happened in there?"

"Dada tried to make nihari," Shaheer said. "Didn't go as planned."

Dad sighed but didn't comment further. Shaheer side-eyed Dad when he didn't head straight for a shower as usual. Instead, he tossed his white coat aside before bending down to dig through his backpack at Shaheer's feet. Shaheer's insides squirmed as he pretended not to notice.

He jolted when Dad dropped a pile of flyers in his lap. *What the—?*

"I picked these up on the way home," Dad said, his tone light. "Check 'em out."

They all had dates and QR codes on them. Puzzled, Shaheer gingerly flipped through the stack like it was going to bite his fingers off. "'Artechouse,'" he said, reading the first flyer out loud. "'Smithsonian.' 'Georgetown Waterfront.' 'Botanic Garden.'"

"These are the top attractions in DC," Dad said happily. "I've been doing my research. Look, there's even a bike trail. I was thinking we could make a day trip there one weekend. Go touring. We didn't get to sight-see in Boston all that much when we lived there. Or Dallas. Or Chicago. Or Seattle."

Shaheer went still, heat crawling up his neck when he finally understood what Dad was suggesting. He wanted to spend time together.

Shaheer bristled. He wasn't interested in playing happy-go-lucky tourist with Dad. No sir. Were they supposed to spend the rest of their lives living a charade? Dad lost in his own fairy tale, believing all was well between them, while Shaheer pined for more? This place was done for, same as the rest, except—

Ashar's face flashed in front of Shaheer like a traffic signal, making his breath hitch. He wasn't surprised Dad hid so much from him given how tight-lipped he was about the divorce.

"Sport?" Dad's hopeful voice cut through Shaheer's train of thought. "What do you say?" Shaheer blinked at his hands. He didn't want to see Dad's heart breaking when he turned him down.

But maybe he didn't have to.

The decision hatched in Shaheer's head, striking him so suddenly that the papers rustled in his lap.

Ashar's brother-swap plan. If Ashar took Shaheer's place, Ashar could do all the Dad bonding time *for* him.

He still had his doubts about the idea, but Shaheer was starting to understand what Ashar was getting at.

Mom didn't know him at all, and Dad didn't know Ashar. People hung on to the things they loved because they were special to them, and they were special because, well, they knew them. Gave them a piece of their heart. Shaheer had seen the Property Brothers literally drag people away from their old homes to move on. It took getting to know a new house to start caring about it. Then they *stayed* for it and all the new memories they would create.

If Shaheer could convince Dad that he wanted to be near Mom, maybe he'd finally stick around in one place long enough for them to put down roots. All he had to do was act like he wanted Mom in his life and Shaheer would get the home he always wanted. Bonus points if having Ashar back gave Dad double the reason not to move away.

It was absurd, but it just might work.

"I'll think about it," Shaheer said. Dad looked relieved he hadn't straight up rejected him. He nodded and went to freshen up, finally leaving Shaheer alone in front of the TV.

"Oh, I love this part." Dada had materialized over Shaheer's shoulder, quiet as a mouse. Like he'd been listening to them this whole time. "The big reveal. Oof. Makes me tear up every time."

For once, Shaheer was too lost in his head to appreciate the episode's most magical moment. "Hey, Dada? Out of everywhere we've been, is there any one place you really wanted to stay?"

Dada was quiet, longer than Shaheer thought was possible. Finally, he said, "No."

"Why not?"

"Because nowhere had that feeling for me." Dada nodded at the happy cryfest happening on the TV. "That feeling of being home." He slid his gaze to Shaheer, his expression a little sad. For a split second, Shaheer wondered if he was thinking about his other grandson. "But every move is another chance at finding it, right?"

Shaheer hoped. If it meant he could finally find his Forever Home, he would switch places with Ashar. Some things weren't always meant to be left behind. Dad had to see that. Shaheer would make him see it.

12
ASHAR

Ashar couldn't find Shaheer anywhere. If Eddie and Ramiz weren't still clowning about his "evil twin," he would've believed yesterday had been a figment of his imagination. It bothered Ashar that Shaheer was probably avoiding school because of *him*. That wasn't the brotherly vibe he was going for. By noon, Ashar still didn't have an update and he'd all but given up. Shaheer's message rang loud and clear.

Until he walked into the auditorium for study hall and spotted Shaheer all the way in the back. Ashar halted in his tracks so abruptly that a girl collided with him.

"Sorry, sorry!" he said hurriedly, and spun around to tear down the aisle. Shaheer balked when he noticed Ashar hurtling toward him. He took one earbud out when his twin plopped down on the seat beside him.

"Hey," said Ashar.

"Hey," Shaheer said.

A beat of silence weighed down the air between them until Ashar asked, "Where have you been? I've been looking all over for you!"

"Got here right before first bell. Dada made me eat breakfast with him before letting me leave."

"That's cool of him," said Ashar.

A hint of emotion snuck through Shaheer's bored expression at Ashar's astonishment. "Yeah. He's great. You'll see when we switch places."

Ashar put his hand on Shaheer's shoulder, but immediately dropped it. The brief touch lingered warmly on Ashar's fingers. "What did you say?"

Shaheer removed his other earbud and turned to face Ashar full on. There was a determined look in his eyes. "I thought about it, and the plan? You're right."

"I always am," Ashar said. Joking aside, he hadn't realized until that moment how nervous he'd been that Shaheer wouldn't be on board. He breathed a little easier now.

"The only way to get through to Mom and Dad is to make sure they can't walk away from us again. Obviously, they're never gonna like each other again, but that's not the point," Shaheer said. "I just want Dad to stop moving. You know. If I don't want to after meeting Mom."

Ashar nodded. "You won't. You're gonna love Mom. And I wanna know Dad. I mean, he won't know the real me since I'll be pretending to be you, but we'll tell them eventually, right?"

"Right. But we're basically strangers. It'll take time," said Shaheer.

Ashar snorted. "Hard to forget. Anyway, we're gonna help each other out. Train the other on how to be him. Here." Ashar tapped the CREATE CONTACT button on his phone and gave it to Shaheer. Shaheer hesitated like he'd never seen a phone before, but eventually punched in his number and handed it back to Ashar. Good timing, too, because their teacher called them to attention. Shaheer took out his science textbook. Ashar noticed it was the edition the honors class used. Huh.

He pulled up Shaheer's number and sent his brother their first ever text.

Ashar: You're in honors science?

Shaheer checked his phone when the notification popped up and typed a response.

Shaheer: Yeah. Dad makes me take it.
Doctors -_-. He helps me with it when he
has time

Lucky, Ashar thought. Shaheer would probably ace
the science section of Arlington's entrance exam.

Ashar: What math are you in?
Shaheer: Pre-algebra
Ashar: HAH! I'm in geometry :)
Shaheer: ???
Ashar: Mom's a high school math teacher.
I've always been ahead. Plus, it ups my
chances of getting into the academy
Shaheer: What academy?
Ashar: Arlington Academy. Only the best
high school in the whole country. It's
supercompetitive to get into. I'm taking the
first part of the entrance exam in November
Shaheer: Sounds intense. Why do you want
to go there?
Ashar: They have the BEST ice hockey team.
Ever heard of the Icecaps? Legends. Some
of the top college teams recruit from there

Shaheer gave Ashar sideways *okay, so what?* eyes.

> **Ashar:** I play ice hockey (go Husky Bladers!)
> and want to go into the NHL one day.
> Eddie and Ramiz are on my team, too. Do
> you watch hockey?
> **Shaheer:** Not a sports person
> **Ashar:** Then what kind of person are you?

Ashar realized after he sent that message that it was a little weird he had asked his own twin such a basic question, but nothing about their situation was normal. The most he could do was make up for lost time. Shaheer didn't respond right away, like he didn't know how to answer. He picked at his lower lip as he mulled it over. Ashar took out a book to make himself look busy in the meantime. Finally, his phone lit up.

> **Shaheer:** You know what HGTV is?
> **Ashar:** Nope. Never heard of it.
> **Shaheer:** House reno channel. Dada
> and I like watching the Property
> Brothers.
> **Ashar:** That's cool . . .

He supposed. Ashar didn't peg Shaheer to be the interior design type, but what did he know? Before Ashar could think of what to say, Shaheer sent him another message.

Shaheer: So ice hockey, huh?

Ashar: Yeah, wanna see? Mom took a video at our last game

Ashar went through his phone's gallery searching for the clip from the end of last season. Instead of attaching it, his finger accidentally hit the play button. Ayoub Mamou's cheering voice boomed from the speakers at a volume that could wake the dead. "YOU SHOW 'EM, ASH!"

A ripple passed through the auditorium. Every face turned around to stare at Ashar. Shaheer shot him a look and Ashar sank in his chair.

My bad, Ashar mouthed. But he swore he saw Shaheer's lips fighting back a grin.

✦ ✦ ✦

The bell for the day's last lunch period sent a swarm of students flooding the hallway, some heading toward the cafeteria and others going back to classrooms to finish off the block.

In the cafeteria, Zohra spotted Shaheer and Ashar from the lunch line and waved her hands over her head to get their attention. Ashar had packed lunch, but he went over to stand in line with Zohra and Shaheer anyway.

Zohra gawked at Shaheer's hair. "Whoa, doppelgänger alert. What happened?"

The easygoing mood from study hall melted away. Shaheer cast Ashar a glare that told him he was still unhappy about the spur-of-the-moment switch yesterday.

"Nothing," Ashar said. Now Shaheer looked skeptical, like, *Nothing? Really?* Normally, Ashar would fill Zohra in on everything that happened, but after their fight yesterday, he wasn't in the mood to share with her.

"Well, you're a dead ringer for Ashar now, Shaheer," Zohra commented. "Everyone's gonna get you guys mixed up."

"We only have two classes together," said Shaheer.

"No fair. I don't have any with either of you. Thanks for keeping me in the loop, Ash," Zohra said wryly, nabbing a lunch tray a little too aggressively. "Don't you think I deserve to know what's going on since I'm the one who brought you guys together in the first place?"

Zohra's tone ticked Ashar off so bad he was down for a screaming match right there in the lunch line. Her ridiculous grudge made no sense! What had he done to deserve this?

"We could've found out about being twins without you forcing us together, you know," Ashar said, poking the bear on purpose. "It's not like we needed you to butt into our business." The air between him and Zohra sizzled so that Shaheer tentatively stepped a safe distance out of the blast zone to request his food from the lunch lady.

Zohra clenched her milk carton with enough force to tear it right open. She bulldozed past Ashar—smacking him hard as she went—to go sit with her friends without a backward glance.

"What was that about?" Shaheer asked as they left the lunch line, him carrying a cheese pizza and assorted fruits.

"Beats me," Ashar said, rubbing his shoulder. "We're not involving her in the plan, by the way. I think the real Zohra got abducted by aliens or something. She's never usually like this."

"Then shouldn't we be worried she'll sell us out to the adults?" Shaheer said.

"Let's hope not," said Ashar.

"Have you tried asking her what's wrong?"

"What for? I didn't do anything!" Ashar exclaimed.

Shaheer's expression was doubtful, but he smartly dropped the subject and set his tray down at the end of an empty table near the kitchen doors. He looked up in surprise when Ashar joined him. "Don't you have somewhere else to sit?" Ashar wasn't sure if that meant Shaheer wanted to be left alone, but he chanced it anyway. They needed to get a few things straight about switching places. And . . . he wanted to spend time with Shaheer. It wasn't every day you learned you had a secret brother.

"No," Ashar said. He took care of his friends' inquisitive looks with a few sneaky texts, then turned back to Shaheer. He jumped right into it. "So, when do we start?"

Shaheer took a long sip of chocolate milk. "Now, I guess? First, we need a game plan. We have to be pretty convincing so that our families don't find out we're tricking them. Maybe we can meet after school and go over everything we need to know," he suggested.

Ashar groaned. "I can't. I have practice on Tuesdays. And Sundays."

Shaheer shrugged. "I'm good with any day, but just FYI, Dad doesn't come home from work until late. He's only off on Thursdays and Sundays."

"That's perfect! We can do our first switch on Thursday," said Ashar.

Shaheer gaped at him. "*This* Thursday? That's only two days away!"

"Oh, come on! How long's it gonna take for us to learn how to act like each other? Look how much we learned just by texting in study hall. And it's not like we're swapping lives *completely*. Just a couple days here and there at home should do it. Wait, we might have to switch phones, too. Or just our cases. Unless we can hide them from Mom and Dad. I don't know, what do you think?" Ashar rambled like if he didn't get all his thoughts on the table, Shaheer would talk himself out of the plan. Ashar just couldn't wait to meet Dad. And back in the auditorium, he and Shaheer had had a real moment. It was like the gap between them closed a little with every message.

But Shaheer dropped Ashar's gaze and the gap opened up again. Man, Ashar really thought them talking had warmed Shaheer up. They hadn't exactly been sharing their deepest, darkest secrets, but he'd thought there'd been something there.

"Okay, how about this?" Ashar said. "Tonight, we both make a list. Write down whatever you think is important for me to know, and I'll do the same. We'll trade tomorrow morning and then talk more about it after school. Deal?"

Ashar held his breath as Shaheer raked a hand through his hair and sighed. "'Kay. Deal."

13
SHAHEER

Shaheer flung a mini hash brown at Ashar's head when he'd had enough. "Ashar, wake up!" he nagged. "This was all your idea. At least try to look like you're paying attention."

"Listen, hockey wiped me out yesterday," he said. "After that I did homework and practice math problems with Mom. Then this." Ashar gestured to the scribble-filled notebook on the Dunkin' table in front of Shaheer and yawned. "I'm a little tired. And why are you pinning everything on me? You agreed to it!"

"Did I?" Shaheer put a finger on his chin like he was fake thinking. "Or am I afraid if I don't, you'll force us to randomly trade places again? Maybe next time, you'll make me take your place at ice hockey."

"Pfft. Not in a million years. And how many times do I have to apologize?" Ashar blew a raspberry. "You sure hold a grudge. You and Zohra should hang out."

"Whatever. Let's get back to this. There's not a lot of time if we're still aiming for tomorrow." Shaheer gulped the last wisps of his iced latte to cool down and flipped through what could be an actual memoir of Ashar's life. Shaheer had jotted his own down in his phone and sent it over text. He had his work cut out for him. Ashar's life was—not boring.

"Is this really it?" Ashar asked about Shaheer's list for the hundredth time. Shaheer nodded. Ashar stared at his phone like he'd been expecting a challenge and it didn't live up. Shaheer hadn't had much to convey except "don't talk so much." Ashar had given him entire character profiles on Mom, Zohra, Ayoub Mamou, Faiza Mami, Ashar's friends in case Mom asked questions, stuff about Mom's job, where things were in the house with an actual *map*. The more Shaheer learned, the more his chest felt like it was being stomped on. This whole other side of his family and life that Dad had kept from him all laid out like that. He felt left out, like he hadn't gotten invited to a close friend's birthday party.

When Ashar had told Shaheer about Arlington

Academy and playing ice hockey, a pang of jealousy had shot through him. Must be nice to have a list this long and detailed. To be part of a team and have a future planned out. Ashar didn't have to cruise on "getting by" mode all the time. Some people had all the luck.

"How do you have time for ice hockey with school and getting ready for the Arlington exam?" Shaheer asked.

Ashar's face changed. He looked down and said, "I can't study as hard as I want for the entrance exam. Mom couldn't afford a tutor *and* to keep me on the team. I chose ice hockey, so now Arlington's all on me."

Oh. Shaheer fiddled with his smartwatch, suddenly feeling the need to take it off and stuff it in his bag. "Why'd you choose hockey?" Shaheer said.

"Because I love it," Ashar said simply. "When I'm on the ice, everything else disappears. I'm not an expert or anything yet, but—man. It's awesome. And the irony is that I only want to go to Arlington because I want to play for the Icecaps. But I can't play for the best ice hockey team if I'm not already setting personal records and getting better."

Shaheer thought about that for a minute. "You want to go to the NHL, right? Do you *have* to be on the Icecaps to do that? Like, is that your only ticket to go pro?"

Ashar fiddled with his sleeve. "It's the fastest way. The longer route is way more expensive because that means more seasons, more practices, more replacing gear and equipment. And do you know how many Muslims play for the NHL? Like, barely any! Ice hockey's *tough*. I guess that's why I enjoy it, because it pushes me to do my best."

Can't relate, Shaheer thought. His brother was the do-it-all type of guy. That was going to be tough to copy.

Ashar's voice lowered. "Hey, you should know. Ever since we moved out of Ayoub Mamou's, Mom hasn't been herself. So, like, don't take it personally if she gets a little grumpy."

"You guys used to live with Zohra's family?"

"Yep. Since the divorce. We moved here with Ayoub Mamou from Jersey when I was four."

Shaheer chewed the inside of his mouth, quelling the dread curling up behind his ribs. "Then I should give you a heads-up about Dad and Dada, too. They get into it sometimes."

Ashar groaned. "About what?"

"I don't know. Just don't mess up. I don't need to find out what their breaking point is. They're all I have." Shaheer hadn't meant to snip or confess like that, but his resolve was wobbling. *Maybe we're in over our heads.* There was so much on both sides that neither of them knew. One mistake and everything would fall apart in the snap of a finger. Shaheer had seen what Ashar was capable of. What if he reacted rashly to something and Dad and Dada found out who he really was? If Ashar really was such a sore spot for Dad and Dada, where would Shaheer go if they couldn't see past their differences and who would he live with then? He wanted his life here to be more than just a long stop to . . . somewhere else. But Dad and Dada were the only constants in his life. Was staying here worth wagering that?

It has to be, Shaheer thought. If Dad wanted to fix things between them that bad, then Shaheer was banking on Dad choosing *him* at the end of the day. Nothing else.

"Do you, Dad, and Dada go to jummah together?" Ashar asked.

The question threw Shaheer off for a second. "You go to the masjid?"

"Yeah. Mom always makes sure we do volunteer work a couple times a month, too. Says it's the least we can do. You don't go?"

Heat prickled the back of Shaheer's neck. "No. Dad's not big on religion. He still wants me to be a better Muslim than him, though. It doesn't make any sense. If he thinks it's so important for me, why doesn't he follow Islam better himself?"

Shaheer waited for the judgy eyes, but Ashar's were sympathetic instead. "Mom gets that way sometimes, too. Like, she'll tell me to revise my surahs, but she won't open the Qur'an for weeks." Ashar shrugged. "Parents aren't perfect just because they're parents. They can make mistakes, too."

Ashar's voice was reachy. Shaheer could tell Ashar wanted him to open up to him. Shaheer didn't think it was smart to go that route yet. He didn't know if the whole swapping-places thing would even convince Dad to stay here. He'd worry about what to do with his brother later. Shaheer was still too wigged out by the fact that he'd had a twin roaming the planet this whole time and didn't even know it.

Ashar's face dropped when Shaheer didn't continue the conversation. Guilt dug its nails into Shaheer's chest for shutting him down. He refocused on Ashar's life story to avoid the awkwardness.

"That's it. I'm screwed. I can't pull this off," Shaheer said, stabbing at the ice clinking at the bottom of his cup with his straw.

"Yes, you can," said Ashar. "You'll be a great me. Mom's gonna love you. Trust me."

But what if Mom *didn't* like him? What if Shaheer liked Mom better than Dad?

Worse, what if Dad liked Ashar better?

14
ASHAR

Ashar and Shaheer barely talked on Thursday, the tension like a taut spring between them. Ashar watched the minutes tick by in agony, his insides icing over as the end of the day neared.

When school let out, they traded all their belongings in the bathroom.

"Make sure you like all of Ramiz's posts," Ashar instructed. "Leave an insult in the comments for good measure. Any last-minute advice for me?" Ashar shouldered Shaheer's backpack, and they left the side entrance to where Shaheer's bike was parked. "Got my address?" asked Ashar.

"Yup."

"Don't forget to take the stuff Mom asked out of the freezer. They're in her last text."

Ashar's fingers wobbled as he tried unlocking the bike cable. After a few unsuccessful attempts, Shaheer blurted, "How hard is it for you to get it open?"

"You do it, then," Ashar said, standing up and wiping his slick palms on Shaheer's jeans.

Shaheer snatched the keys from him, and the cable fell away in one swift motion.

"Show-off," muttered Ashar.

Ashar and Shaheer stared at each other over the bike seat. Shaheer stuffed his hands into his pockets, the only sign that he was feeling uneasy. "I guess this is it," Shaheer said. "We're really doing this. Good luck. Keep me posted if there's an emergency."

Ashar wanted to hug him, but he didn't think Shaheer was about that. He opted for two thumbs up instead. "See ya tomorrow." Then he mounted Shaheer's bike and pedaled away.

◆ ◆ ◆

Ashar wasn't sure if the sweat accumulating on his forehead was from the bike ride under the stifling sun or from nerves. He stood in front of the door to Shaheer's apartment long enough for it to look suspicious. At least he wasn't banging down the door this time.

Dad was on the other side. After all this time, he was so close. There was no going back once he stepped through that door. He let the thought settle into his bones before gathering up the courage to use Shaheer's key to open the door.

A flood of Urdu curse words reached his ear through the crack, followed by the sound of something metal hitting the floor. Then the *smell* greeted his nostrils.

"Abba, let me do it," someone said.

"I got this!" said another, gruffer voice. "Get out of the kitchen. Go iron your coats. They have more wrinkles than me."

Ashar's eyes fogged with tears and he coughed into his hand. That and the door slamming made the two men in the kitchen snap their heads up at him.

"Assalamualaikum," said Dada, looking the same as he had the last time. Ashar let his bag and helmet fall to the ground as he absorbed what was in front of him. Dad, looking like he just rolled out of bed in George Washington University Hospital T-shirt and sweatpants, waved at him over the counter. Ashar's heart raced. *Oh my God. He looks like me. I look like him.* They were like one of those three-generation photos that went viral on social media.

"What's up?" said Dad.

Ashar gulped back the air lodged in his throat, his eyes glued to Dad. *Get it together*, he berated himself. *Shaheer wouldn't cry.*

The tears flowed unchecked anyway and the voice inside his head that sounded vaguely like Shaheer begging him to pull it together got shoved into the background.

"Shaheer! Kya hua?" Dada came around to kneel in front of him, the lines around his eyes creasing even more as Ashar's sobbing intensified. Dada took his face in his hands. "Are you hurt? Jawad, what's wrong with him?"

"Hey, what's going on, sport?" Dad joined Dada. "Did something happen at school?"

Shaheer wouldn't do what he was about to, but Ashar didn't care. He launched himself at Dad's neck with such force that Ashar almost toppled him over. Dad smelled like expensive cologne and disinfectant. Ashar breathed it in to calm his erratic emotions as Dad put his arms around him.

"Does he have a fever?" Dada whispered. "Should we take him to the ER?"

That got Ashar's attention. He broke the hug. "No! I'm—I'm okay," he said, hastily swiping at his tears. "I was just, uh, doing an experiment."

"An experiment?" said Dad.

"Yeah. A science experiment. I go up to people and start crying to see what they do. I was gonna make up my answer, but I wanted to know how you guys would react." Ashar cringed at how fake he sounded.

"That sounds like a social experiment," Dad said slowly. Well, how was Ashar supposed to know that? "Are they offering psychology in middle school now?"

"Oh, for heaven's sake," Dada groaned, standing up. "You win, Jawad. Place an order. I'm going to take a shower. And please open the windows. The smell is foul," he called over his shoulder on his way to the bathroom.

"What got ruined?" Ashar asked. Now that he was done embarrassing himself, he focused on making his voice sound more like Shaheer's. Casual, indifferent.

"I don't even know what he was trying to make," Dad said, going around to crack all the windows. "I heard a commotion right before you got in. Woke me up from my nap." Dad put his hands on his hips and surveyed the living room like he was rating the quality of fresh air. Content, he spun back to face Ashar. "What are you feeling for dinner?"

"Like from anywhere?" Ashar lit up inside. He and Mom rarely ate out. First, it was extra money. Second, she thought it was unhealthy.

"Unless you want to eat whatever that is," Dad said, nodding toward the kitchen.

"No, thanks." Ashar thought about it. What would Shaheer choose? He went with the safest bet. "Pizza?"

"Sure. Let me do that right now." Dad whipped out his phone. "The usual?"

Ashar hesitated before saying yes. He hoped the "usual" was halal.

Dad sprawled on the sofa as he filled out the order on the app. "Dada tells me you've been hanging out with some kids at school."

"He did?"

"Mhm. Sorry we haven't really gotten the chance to catch up about your first few days. Busy shifts."

"Guess you needed that nap, huh?" said Ashar.

"I always need a nap. But I have time now." Dad flicked his eyes at him. Shaheer would use homework as an excuse and ditch. But wasn't getting to know Dad the whole reason why he was here? What would be the point of locking himself up in Shaheer's room?

Think, Ashar. Think.

"That's a first," Ashar said, grabbing his bag on the way to the breakfast table. He smiled to himself. That'd been a pretty good impersonation of his brother. Ashar kept his back turned to give the illusion that he wasn't completely interested as he opened Shaheer's agenda to check for homework. Today's date was blank. Oh-kay. As Ashar was lifting the science textbook out to pretend to read it, his—well, Shaheer's—phone buzzed. It was a little creepy to be getting a message from his own number.

> **Shaheer:** How's it going?
>
> **Ashar:** Good
>
> **Shaheer:** Really?
>
> **Ashar:** OK, I might've ugly cried, but I handled it like a boss. They didn't suspect a thing
>
> **Shaheer:** Way to go
>
> **Ashar:** What are your usual pizza toppings?

Ashar waited for a reply, but Shaheer decided to ghost him after that. Dad sat down across from Ashar at the table, and he fumbled with the phone like he'd been caught doing something illegal. Stealing someone else's identity *was* illegal, he supposed.

"What do you think of Virginia so far?" Dad asked, brushing off Ashar's previous comment. Ashar was starting to see where Shaheer got his couldn't-care-less attitude from.

Ashar shrugged, quietly panicking as he flipped to a random chapter. He didn't know the first thing about the places they used to live before. "It's nice, I guess. A lotta . . . trees." Ashar wanted to bang his head on the table.

"The greenery's nice. DC's not bad for a big city." Ashar didn't respond, but he got the sense that there was more to it than that. Like they were communicating in some secret code. One that Ashar didn't know how to crack because Shaheer's notes were lousy and not helping him at all right now!

After a stretched silence, Dad said, "So, have you thought about what I said?"

About what? What is he talking about?! Ashar felt like he was about to burst at the seams.

"Shaheer? Are you okay? You look kind of sick."

"Totally fine!" Ashar piped up. "Just reading about"—he peered at the chapter title—"force, motion, and energy." *Oh no.*

"Physical science," said Dad. "Never liked it. Or earth science. Bio and chem are where it's at. But I'm biased," he added good-naturedly. "I can still be of help, though."

The science talk was beginning to make Ashar dizzy when a memory niggled at his brain—Shaheer saying that Dad helped him with science when he had time.

A light bulb went off in Ashar's head. Dad was a science buff. Science was Ashar's worst subject. What if *Dad* could help him study for the Arlington exam? With Mom preparing him in math and Dad tutoring him in science, Ashar could have a shot at the Icecaps after all!

"Dad?" Ashar said.

"Yes, sport?"

"Can you help me go over some practice questions? I want to make sure I remember everything from sixth and seventh grade. You know, for the SOL. In Virginia, eighth grade is the only year in middle school we take the standardized test in science."

"Of course," said Dad. He looked genuinely happy. "Just let me know what you need."

Ashar's throat thickened again, but he was saved by a knock at the door and Dad going to get it.

Ashar was glad Dad had said yes, but he didn't want tutoring to be the only thing he and Dad did together, though. Ashar remembered Shaheer telling him Dad had Sundays off, too. But on Sundays . . . he had ice hockey. As soon as that realization hit him, though, another much wilder idea sprouted. Beyond wild.

The smell of pizza filled the apartment, and Ashar put the thought away to discuss with Shaheer tomorrow.

Ashar opened the box with his mouth watering. "EWW!" He accidentally gagged out loud.

"What? Did they get our order wrong?" Dad peered at the box. "Looks right to me. What's wrong? I thought this was your favorite?"

Ashar swallowed the bile rising in his throat. "Thought I saw a dead bug. All good," he mumbled. He slapped the lid shut and punched out a message to Shaheer.

Ashar: You put spinach and pineapple on your pizza?? We need to have a serious TALK!!

15
SHAHEER

The fridge in Ashar and Mom's town house was covered in colorful magnets and school pictures of Ashar over the years and little notes from Mom's students. They'd moved in less than a month ago, but there was already this warmth Shaheer had never felt before. Who cared if the hardwood floors weren't as shiny, the walls were different colors, and the kitchen was super outdated? It *felt* like a home, and he used the time before Mom returned to inspect every inch of it hungrily.

In the powder room, Shaheer froze when he heard the front door click and overlapping voices traveled inside.

"Careful, Papa." Zohra's voice nearly sent Shaheer toppling face-first into the toilet. "The corner's tearing on that one."

Zohra! What was she doing here? He hadn't been expecting the whole gang to show up!

Shaheer tore himself away from the bathroom and stumbled over to the sitting room next to the kitchen. His knee painfully hit the corner of the coffee table and he went down in a silent scream as Mom, Zohra, and a man that could only be Ayoub Mamou came into view.

"Assalamualaikum," Mom said, giving him a full-wattage grin. Shaheer's breath caught. Round face, long midnight-black hair, brown eyes rimmed with thick lashes. She was beautiful. Shaheer could've stared forever if his knee wasn't killing him.

"What's with you?" Zohra asked, raising one eyebrow at Shaheer sprawled on the rug.

"Uh—nothing. What brings you here?" Zohra scrunched up her face like she'd bitten straight into a lemon. What? What had he said wrong?

Ayoub Mamou gestured to the overstuffed box in his hands. Ugh. Cardboard. "We're just helping Zareena bring some last-minute stuff over that was still sitting in our storage."

Mom set the box down at her feet and dug through it. "Look what I found, Ash. Your blankie. Aw, you slept with this until you were seven." Shaheer froze when he got a good look at the blanket. He recognized its stars-and-clouds pattern. He'd had one just like it as a baby, except where Ashar's was blue and yellow, his had been green and gray.

That settled it. This was all real. If there was any doubt before, it all vanished into thin air now. The enormousness of what he was doing, where he was, hit Shaheer like a truck.

A slow wave of heat like that one blistering summer they'd spent in Texas fanned out from his core to every inch of his skin. One thought kept turning in his head nonstop.

Mom had deserted him. So why was he here, trying to include himself where he wasn't wanted? Why was he the one making the first move?

Forget it, Shaheer. Mom clearly didn't care about him, so it wasn't worth being mad over. She was just a means to an end. Dad just needed to *think* Shaheer wanted to keep her around if he was going to persuade him not to move again. And he couldn't convince Dad of that if he sensed that Shaheer wasn't being sincere. Shaheer would just have to accept whatever had happened in the past and focus on the now.

"Do you mind if I donate it? The cloth is in good shape, if a little faded."

Mom's voice snapped Shaheer out of it. He shrugged like *do whatever you want.*

Mom sized Shaheer up as if his reaction surprised her. "Thought you'd put up more of a fight," she said. Shaheer suspected Ashar *would* have, but sadly, there seemed to be gum sticking Shaheer's mouth shut, so he was relieved when Mom kept on. "But I'm glad you're okay parting with it. We can add it to the pile of donations."

"What donations?" Oh, *now* he decided to speak.

"For the drive to set up the new masjid they're opening?" Mom said. Not helping. She didn't look pleased at the blank look on Shaheer's face. *At least act like you know what she's talking about!* But all his senses appeared to have fled.

"Ash, we agreed that no matter how busy we are, we have to contribute some time to our community," said Mom. "Ayoub Mamou offered to help transport things since people are dropping stuff off at his house all week. We're going to need your and Zohra's help sorting through all the items and determining what's useful."

"How's that useful?" Zohra pointed at Ashar's blanket.

"I was thinking it could be sewn into a kid-sized hijab. It's always a good idea to keep extra things like that on hand in case someone needs to borrow it." Mom looked to Shaheer like he might offer a different idea. As if he knew anything about setting up a masjid. When was the last time he'd been? Eight, nine years old?

Mom's eyes traveled down to Shaheer's hand, and her mouth scrunched up. "Where did you get that, Ash?"

Shaheer felt at his hand and went cold. Oh *no*. He'd forgotten to take off his smartwatch!

"That's not yours," said Mom.

Shaheer went stone still. His mind ransacked through a hundred different excuses like a broken wheel of misfortune. Zohra's gaze slid from Shaheer's wrist slowly up to his face, her eyes narrowing behind her glasses as they settled on him with suspicion.

"Ashar," Mom said sternly. "I don't want to assume the worst, so please explain."

"I didn't steal it!" Shaheer finally said. "It's—" Crap! What were Ashar's friends' names again? "Eddie! It's Eddie's. He asked me to hold on to it for him and I forgot to give it back."

Mom eased up. "Well, make sure you return it

tomorrow. Bhai, are you eating with us? I made beef koftay."

"As much as I love your koftay, we can't. Faiza's already made dinner," said Ayoub Mamou.

"Can we please stay for just a little while?" Zohra asked while Shaheer thought, *Yeah, please go away.*

Ayoub Mamou sighed, but Shaheer got the feeling the decision wasn't hard for him. "Fine. Only a little taste."

"We're gonna go put these boxes in the basement. In the meantime, can you and Zohra warm up—where's the naan?" Mom asked, her eyes scanning the kitchen. "Ashar, I asked you to take them out of the freezer before I left school."

And Ashar had reminded him, too. This was going swell.

"Sorry," Shaheer mumbled.

Mom sighed like she was disappointed. "All right, it will take a few extra minutes. Reheat the pot, too, please."

"Sure thing," Zohra said. She whirled on Shaheer when their parents' voices faded down the steps. "Why do you have Shaheer's watch?" she deadpanned.

"None of your business," Shaheer said, rolling up his sleeves and sauntering over to the kitchen. Ashar and Zohra were supposedly arguing, so he thought his response was dead-on. He regretted it when he opened the jam-packed freezer and remembered he had no clue how to warm up naan.

Zohra planted her elbows on the kitchen counter and watched as Shaheer floundered. "Problem? You're acting like you've never done this before."

Great. Should he come clean to Zohra or risk burning down the whole house? Ashar had said he didn't want her to be in the know, and since Shaheer knew virtually zilch about his cousin, he didn't know what to do.

"Shaheer."

"What?" he replied automatically, and blanched when he realized his mistake a split second later.

"I knew it!" Zohra exclaimed, picking herself up half off the bar stool. "What do you think you're doing here? Where's Ashar?"

"Quiet down!" Shaheer pleaded, gesturing pointedly toward the basement stairs.

"Answer my question first," said Zohra.

Shaheer sighed. There was no point in lying to her now. All he could do was hope Ashar didn't chew him out for it tomorrow. "Ashar's with Dad pretending to be me."

Zohra stared at him like he'd sprouted a tail and whiskers. "Why?"

Shaheer quickly filled her in on Ashar's fumble in front of Dada and the whole brother-swap plan in a low voice, half his attention trained toward the basement in case Mom and Ayoub Mamou came back.

"Freaking Ashar!" Zohra seethed when Shaheer was finished. "I can't believe he pulled that stunt behind my back! When I get my hands on him—"

"Look, I don't know what your guys' problem is, but right now I could really use some help," Shaheer said. "We don't do a lot of cooking at our house."

"Fine. Only because I feel bad for you." Zohra demonstrated how to wrap the naan in aluminum foil before sticking them in the oven. Then she had Shaheer turn the burner below the pot to medium-high heat. Shaheer lifted the lid and took a sniff of the koftay. He immediately spun around and sneezed into his arm.

"Gross!" Zohra said. "Keep your germs away from that."

"It's so spicy!" Shaheer complained.

Zohra gave him a withering look. "Ashar likes spicy food. Just pinch your nose and swallow it. If you're gonna fool Papa and Zareena Phuppo, then you need to not be so terrible at this," she hissed. "Do better or you're gonna blow your cover!"

Shaheer wanted to defend himself, but Zohra was right. He couldn't chance Mom finding out who he really was, or it would ruin everything. Plus, he needed to stay on Zohra's good side if he wanted her to cover for him. She would make sure that he was always channeling his inner Ashar since she knew him better than anyone. He'd already made too many mistakes.

Shaheer was grumbling about what he'd gotten himself into when Mom and Ayoub Mamou reappeared. As they got the food ready and chatted, Shaheer tried making more of an effort to participate, mostly following Zohra's lead. Ayoub Mamou's glasses and playful eyes reminded him of Zohra, which was comforting. But the longer he was around Mom, the more Shaheer's shoulders tensed. She whipped around the kitchen like a tornado, not noticing anything off about her son.

The thought weighed Shaheer down, and a strange feeling climbed his throat. Shaheer had never felt so . . . erased. He was used to it in a way, but this was different. There was Mom standing right in front of him, but she thought he was Ashar. Shaheer was her son, too, but not the one she'd wanted to keep. What would she say if she knew he was standing there? What about Ayoub Mamou?

Shaheer's mind pinwheeled as he took in the people standing around him. His mom. His uncle. His cousin. Pieces that'd been missing from his life for so long, and now that he'd found them, he didn't know where they fit or how to make them fit. And where did that leave him?

I don't know if I can do this.

Shaheer texted Ashar when no one was looking.

> **Shaheer:** What are you doing rn?
>
> **Ashar:** Eating pizza >:(These toppings should be illegal
>
> **Shaheer:** I have to eat level 10 spicy meatballs for you
>
> **Ashar:** No fair!! Trade ya

"When's your first game, Ash?" Ayoub Mamou asked when they sat down to eat. "More importantly, when are you playing against those hooligans? The Cardinal Jetters."

Shaheer silently thanked Ashar for being an over-achiever. He remembered from his notes that Ayoub Mamou was the one who'd introduced him to ice hockey, and that the Cardinal Jetters are the Husky Bladers biggest rivals.

Shaheer's gaze kept going to Mom like she had all the answers. "Don't know yet. Coach Taylor wants us to take it one game at time."

"I'm looking forward to that one," Mom said. "To watching you guys crush them, that is."

"You mean like how the Cardinals crushed them last time?" Zohra said. She looked at Shaheer apologetically. "Sorry, Ash."

"Not this time," Shaheer said. "We're gonna beat them. Just wait. I'll even score the winning goal." Shaheer wanted to take those words back almost immediately. Talk about *over*confident. Zohra's side-eye was approving, though.

"That's the spirit!" Ayoub Mamou said, ripping a naan in half.

"By the way, you're all signed up for the Arlington exam in November," said Mom. "They'll send us more information a few weeks before. Don't stress," she added, patting Shaheer's arm. "I have some grading to do tonight, but we can keep working on the math later."

Shaheer cleared his throat. "Works for me."

"You haven't touched your food."

Shaheer couldn't weasel his way out of this one, so he tore off a piece of naan, dipped it in the meatball curry, and slowly brought it to his mouth. Hot flavor sizzled his tongue.

"I'll pack some for you to take for bhabi," Mom told Ayoub Mamou. "What does everyone think?" Ayoub Mamou and Zohra complimented the food earnestly.

Shaheer gave her a thumbs-up, his eyes watering dramatically. "So good. Thanks, Mom."

16
ASHAR

Ashar caught up to Shaheer leaving the auditorium on Friday morning as he flew through the doors just in time for first bell.

Shaheer looked dead on his feet. "Overslept?" he said so only Ashar could hear as they walked together toward their lockers. "I'm jealous. Mom woke me up for Fajr. Too early," he complained with droopy eyelids.

"I had to sneak into the bathroom to make wudu this morning," Ashar said in a low voice. "Dada caught me. I lied and said I was having tummy aches."

Shaheer snorted. "My stomach *actually* hurt all night! Do you know how long I was on the toilet?"

"TMI," Ashar gagged.

They split in House A. Ashar remembered he still had

Shaheer's backpack, but that wasn't an issue since they were in the same first block. Next time, though, it was probably smarter to keep their own books. Ashar was not about to do Shaheer's brainiac science homework.

Ashar turned to go find Shaheer. He was itching to know how it had gone with Mom, but Eddie and Ramiz appeared on either side of him.

"He almost had us this time, but not because of the haircut," Eddie said, tilting his chin in Shaheer's direction. Ashar followed Eddie's line of sight to— Uhh, why was Zohra talking to Shaheer? Why was she *whispering* to Shaheer from behind her hand like that?

"First your look, now your cousin. Next thing you know, he's abducting you and taking over your life," Ramiz joked.

Ha. Ha. If they only knew.

Ashar told Eddie and Ramiz he'd find them later and strode over to Zohra and Shaheer. Shaheer averted his attention to the wall clock like the time had suddenly piqued his interest, but Zohra just leaned back against the wall of lockers and pinned him with flinty eyes.

"Hey, Ashar," she said. "Or should I say Shaheer. Whoever you are today."

Ashar stopped in his tracks. Ten seconds of dead air

followed before he whirled on Shaheer. "You *told* her?" he griped.

Shaheer blew out a quiet rush of air like he wished he could be anywhere else right now. "No. Yes. I might've slipped up when Mom and Ayoub Mamou weren't around," he admitted.

"Thanks for cluing me in," Zohra said through gnashed teeth. "So much for being family."

Heat zipped through Ashar's body. "Speak for yourself! Not like you've been great at that lately either." Ashar recalled the way Zohra went from being closer than a sister to every single one of her snubs and snide remarks in the last couple of weeks with zero explanation, and he channeled all that rage at Shaheer. "You should've asked me first! I told you I didn't want her in on it."

Zohra looked ready to drop-kick Ashar in the middle of House A.

"What part of 'I messed up' did you not get? Zohra and Ayoub Mamou showed up at the house and it threw me off." Shaheer put his hands up at Ashar's hardened expression. "You need to cool it. Zohra had my back."

"Yeah," Zohra scoffed. "You'd think he'd know me better."

"No offense, but you are being kind of extra," Shaheer agreed.

Ashar felt like he was in the middle of a game where the other team's players were ganging up on him with no backup. He mussed the front of his hair in agitation. "I can't believe you screwed up on our first try!"

"Don't act like *you* did such a fantastic job. Crybaby," Shaheer mumbled.

"A fact," Zohra snickered.

"Really?" Ashar yelled loud enough that several people side-eyed him.

"Stop it," Shaheer said, shutting his locker. "Just forget it. Tell me what happened yesterday," he prompted.

Ashar glowered at Zohra, thinking she'd take that as her cue to leave. Zohra folded her arms at Ashar as if daring him to force her out. Ashar relented since it didn't appear Shaheer was gonna take his side.

"You first," said Ashar.

Shaheer sighed. "Fine. After Zohra and Ayoub Mamou left, Mom and I hung out downstairs. She was grading and I did my homework on the couch. We didn't say much, but . . . it was okay. I watched TV."

"You watched *TV* with Mom sitting right there?"

Ashar said. Shaheer didn't sound like he was super pumped about meeting Mom, and that made Ashar nervous. "Did something bad happen? Was Mom, you know, okay?"

"She was fine," said Shaheer. Ashar noticed a strange look enter Shaheer's eyes, but he didn't go into more detail. Weird.

"Okay, well. Dad was not what I expected," said Ashar. "The whole time I was scared he would figure out it was me and kick me out. But he wasn't mean at all. Like, I thought I'd be mad at him for bailing on us, but it never happened."

Shaheer looked like he was going to say something to that, but then he narrowed his eyes at Ashar. "Why do you have that look on your face?"

"That's his up-to-no-good face," said Zohra.

Ashar laughed nervously and Shaheer glared at him. "What did you do, Ashar?"

"So—can you skate? Know how to hold a hockey stick?"

"Why?" Shaheer asked, his face contorting in confusion.

"Funny thing. You know how Dad's really good at science and how I need help studying for the science material on the Arlington exam?" Shaheer was impassive as other eighth graders milled around them in a medley of loud chatter and hushed gossip, but Ashar saw him grip his backpack strap like he was bracing himself for impact.

"I might've asked Dad to tutor me. Since he's free on Thursdays and Sundays, I thought hey, why don't I spend both days with him? Thursdays for learning, Sundays to have fun, and youcangotopracticepretendingtobeme." The last part came out sounding like his words were being put through a food processor.

Shaheer did not look amused. "What did you say?" he said through gritted teeth.

"I told you he was up to no good," Zohra muttered.

"Shut up, Zohra. That's a yes, right?" Ashar said, whacking Shaheer's shoulder.

"No! Are you serious?" Shaheer snapped, cheeks coloring. "How did you go from 'not in a million years' to 'Shaheer should totally cover for me at ice hockey! *Yeet!*'?"

"Hey, the whole point is for me to get to know him, right?" Ashar retorted. "I can't do that if I only get one day with him! It's not my fault his schedule sucks."

"I don't know how to play ice hockey! I don't even know how ice hockey *works!*"

"I'll teach you." Ashar said it as easily as if he were offering to train Shaheer on how to bake cookies and not how to play a whole competitive team sport. Ashar knew it was a risk. Giving up one day of practice every week meant less time on the ice and losing out on improving his chops at a faster rate, but he was a better hockey player than he was a science student. He would manage. "Come on, Shaheer. Please? I don't wanna skip practice and look bad."

"Are you out of your mind? You think your coach and teammates won't notice if you suddenly suck? Eddie and Ramiz?"

"It's only for one hour on Sundays," Ashar begged. "And that's usually the day we focus on fitness and team strategizing. There's not a whole lot of skating. Sometimes we do a team bonding exercise off-rink. There's a good chance you won't get stuck with actual hockey. *Please?*"

Shaheer groaned. "Would it be so bad if you don't get into Arlington? It's just like any other school. I've been to several. They're literally all the same. I don't see why high school would be any different."

Ashar gave Shaheer a look that suggested he had asked him an impossible question. "Arlington is my best and quickest chance at reaching the NHL. I have to get in."

Shaheer's eye twitched as he struggled to keep his composure. Warring expressions chased themselves across the planes of his face. Shaheer wasn't telling him the whole story. Ashar could tell something else was bothering him, but what?

"Sorry, that's not my problem," Shaheer finally said. "Sometimes things don't always work out the way we want. Maybe you shouldn't get your hopes up. My suggestion—play for a regular high school's team. You'll stand out more."

Shaheer took out last night's reading assignment and flipped over the page of literary analysis questions like he hadn't just stomped all over Ashar's dreams.

"Did you get number four?" Shaheer asked nonchalantly.

Ashar blinked and some of the shock loosened from his lips. "Wait. No? You won't take my place?"

"That's what I said. And if you want to spend more time with Dad, there are other ways. We'll figure it out."

But Ashar wouldn't be able to bond with Dad, *and* get science tutoring, *and* still retain his position on the Husky Bladers. Why couldn't Shaheer see how important this was to him? What kind of brother was he?

"Ashar, hello, hey?" Shaheer's outstretched hand was in his face. "I said can I have my AirPods back now?"

Ashar numbly reached for them in his pocket—then

stopped. Maybe later, he would regret what he was about to do. He was also still ticked off about Shaheer taking Zohra's side over his, but there was too much riding on Shaheer's cooperation. If Ashar couldn't sweet-talk him into taking his place during Sunday practices, then he would make him.

"You want them?" he asked. "Come and get 'em!" Shaheer barely had time to react before Ashar took off in the other direction. Zohra shouted something unintelligible just as Shaheer came to his senses and gave chase like Ashar knew he would. It didn't take a genius to figure out that Shaheer's headphones were his lifeline, especially at school.

"Ashar!" Shaheer cried. "Where do you think you're going? Give me those!"

The commotion drew everyone's attention. Ashar zigzagged between bodies and backpacks as he burst out of House A and streaked down the hallway past seventh graders in House B with Shaheer on his tail.

"Take my place at hockey and I'll give them back!" Ashar bargained over his shoulder.

"ASHAR, I SWEAR I'LL KILL YOU!" Shaheer cried, his hair flying back from his face.

"Boys, no running in the hall—OH!" Principal

Coggins jumped ten feet in the air as Ashar blew past her, making nearby seventh graders cackle. Students had their phones out and were recording with wide grins.

"Get back here!" exclaimed Shaheer.

Ashar screeched to a halt behind one of the long tables inside the empty cafeteria. Just then, the warning bell blared. Ashar had exactly two minutes, or Mr. Burnes would give them both lunch detention for being late to class.

Shaheer spilled inside and bent over with his hands on his knees. His face was as red as a tomato, both from the run and how mad he was. "You. Are. Such. A. Brat," he panted.

Ashar held out Shaheer's AirPods tauntingly across the table. "Say yes or I'll throw them in the trash can. You'll be picking today's breakfast special out of your ears for days."

Shaheer's jaw dropped. "Don't. You. *Dare!*" His voice cracked when he said that. There was that glimmer of something in his expression again.

Ashar stood his ground, scooting closer to the large garbage bins in the middle of the room to prove that he was being serious.

"Okay, fine. Fine! You win. I'll take your place on

Sundays," said Shaheer. He gusted out a long, drawn-out breath. "But just so we're clear, I am *not* playing for you at a real game."

"Heck no. I'm not that desperate. Just stay clear of Coach Taylor. Don't stick out too much." Victorious, Ashar pitched the case in an arc over to Shaheer, who caught it against his chest with a look of displeasure.

"You sure are protective of those things," Ashar remarked. "Was Dad really gonna be mad if you lost them? He could buy you new ones easy."

Shaheer had turned to go, but he whirled back to glower at Ashar. "These *things* were a gift Dad gave me when I turned nine, which was the last birthday that he actually spent with me at home. After that, he was always working."

Ashar watched Shaheer stalk out of the cafeteria, his mouth hanging open but no sound coming out. Even if he had been able to speak, Ashar had no idea what he was supposed to say to that.

17
SHAHEER

Ashar owes me big-time, Shaheer thought as the hockey puck slashed across the ice at him with a vengeance.

It didn't matter how long Ashar spent explaining the rules of the game or showing Shaheer NHL highlights on YouTube until Shaheer's head burst from information overload. Nothing could've prepared him for the real deal. Especially when he'd been expecting the more laid-back Sunday sessions Ashar had sworn would allow him to take it easy and lie low.

So much for that. Apparently, Coach Taylor didn't have the same idea when he woke up this morning.

Shaheer ducked for dear life and lost his balance. He landed hard on his butt with a yelp just as Sohaib sailed over and peered down his nose at him. His eyes were straight fire. This was not the first time Shaheer had mucked up in the last forty-five minutes, and Sohaib's patience was definitely skating on thin ice (pun intended).

"What's gotten into you?" Sohaib snipped. "That was such an easy pass!" The sound of scratching steel blades filled the rink's wintry air around them. Shaheer had difficulty breathing through the layers of gear. He wanted to scratch in a very uncomfortable spot that he couldn't reach through all the padding. *Can't believe Ashar finds this fun. Can't believe he wants to make a career out of this.* The more Shaheer learned about his brother, the more he was starting to think their relation was a fluke.

Shaheer's legs wobbled as he raised himself up, using his hockey stick for support. "Sorry," he ground out. "Off my game today." All Shaheer had managed to do so far was careen into walls and thwack a couple of legs. His brain had decided to dump Ashar's instructions into a mental recycling bin.

"I know last week we told you to have a plan, but doing nothing isn't a plan," said a disgruntled Sohaib. "Get it together. Our first game is next week and right now, you're our weakest link." Jeez, this guy took everything too seriously. Seemed like all he did was harp on everyone's mistakes.

Coach Taylor's whistle ordered them to keep it moving. Sohaib took off without another word. Shaheer gripped his stick with purpose and carefully maneuvered his way into position. At the signal, he marched forward with his eyes on the prize.

"Ash, you're going the wrong way!"

Shaheer slowed, baffled, and drifted halfway around — which set him directly in Jamal's path. Stars burst behind Shaheer's eyes as the boys slammed sides and fell to the ground in a heap.

Sohaib threw up his hands like *I give up!* "We're gonna be the laughingstock of the whole league!" he ranted. "At this rate, we don't stand a chance against the Cardinals."

"We're not playing the Cardinals next week," Coach Taylor said as the whole team flocked to him at the rink's perimeter. Coach Taylor radiated Dwayne "The Rock" Johnson meets robot vibes. Shaheer was terrified of him. He couldn't tell if Coach Taylor was mad as he sized him up.

"Malik, everything all right with you? That was rough."

Shaheer's cheeks burned when the others regarded him with barely concealed disappointment.

"Yes, Coach," he said meekly.

To Shaheer's immense relief, Coach Taylor didn't push

him. After some criticisms, praise, and a pep talk, he let them go.

Shaheer avoided the other guys in the locker room as he lugged off his gear. He took a big gulp of air once he got rid of his helmet. A cramp was puncturing his side and, oh God, his feet hurt worse. He had not signed up for this.

"Yo, Ashar." Ramiz plopped down on the bench next to Shaheer. "What happened out there? I've never seen you play like that."

"Sorry, um, guess I was distracted," Shaheer said, his hands shaking as he redid the laces on his sneakers. "I just have a lot going on."

"You mean with the Arlington entrance exam? Don't sweat it, dude. You'll get in. I know it," Ramiz said, sounding like he really believed it. "But you kind of need to be alive to go there. Just saying." Ramiz smiled.

Shaheer forced a short laugh, then packed up quickly. He felt bad for ditching when the other boy was only trying to help, but he didn't want to stick around too long and expose himself.

Trading places on a Sunday had not been as easy as it was at school on Thursday. They had to make up a story to their parents about meeting up with classmates to do a "semester-long group project." Ashar and Shaheer hung out at the town center bagel shop for an hour before exchanging their stuff and parting ways. Shaheer didn't talk much. He wanted to make sure Ashar knew he was still angry with him for roping him into this. Not only that, but Ashar had stolen Dad's only other free day from Shaheer.

It was the first thing that had popped into Shaheer's head when Ashar proposed they switch places on Sundays. Shaheer didn't understand why it bothered him so much. *He* was the one who didn't want to do all the sightseeing trips in the first place, but it still felt wrong not to see Dad at all.

Shaheer closed the locker door and waved goodbye to Ramiz. He was beginning to wonder if a Forever Home was worth all this trouble.

◆ ◆ ◆

Shaheer was wiped out after an hour on the rink. All he wanted to do was crash in Ashar's bed when they got back, but Mom had other plans.

Instead of going home, they were standing in the gravel parking area of the most run-down-looking house Shaheer had ever seen. Peeling white paint, broken windows on the second floor, weeds growing out of cracks on the front patio.

"The Leesburg Muslim Community Center," said

Mom. "This is the new masjid that needs help setting up before the grand opening."

Help was an understatement. Shaheer had seen plenty of masjids—from big new ones to smaller cozier ones—but nothing like this. It was gonna take a lot more than a fresh coat of paint to fix this disaster. Plus, it was in the middle of nowhere. They'd turned onto the property from a one-way road. Other than a small airport he'd seen on the way here, there was just empty green grass as far as the eye could see.

"It looks . . . creepy," Shaheer said.

"They've been struggling to obtain a permit to build a masjid in this community," Mom explained. "And the previous owner was in a hurry to sell, so a couple of families pitched in and acquired this land. They have big plans to renovate and expand once funds are available, but for now, they're gonna work with what they have. The first step is opening the doors for prayer and Sunday school. Your mamou will be here any minute with all the donations. I hope you saved some energy."

Right at that moment, a huge pickup truck and a white SUV rumbled into the parking lot. Ayoub Mamou and Zohra emerged from the truck and a tall woman in sunglasses stepped out of the SUV.

"Borrowed this from a neighbor," Ayoub Mamou said,

patting the truck's hood. "Couldn't fit everything into our car."

"The response has been amazing," the woman said, coming up to them. Shaheer figured this was Zohra's mom, Faiza Mami. "We might even have *too* much stuff. I'm not sure it will all fit."

"We can stack extra stuff in storage," said Mom. "You never know when something might come in handy."

Zohra's gaze slid over Shaheer knowingly before she asked, "Is it just us?"

"A few other people said they were coming," said Ayoub Mamou. He jiggled a set of keys. "But we're not waiting. Let's head inside first."

The short set of stairs leading up to the front door creaked like it was going to collapse under their weight. Ayoub Mamou turned the key and pushed—nothing. He had to shove the door with his shoulder a couple of times before it finally unstuck. He walked in and flipped the lights on. To Shaheer's surprise, the inside was almost new-ish. The main floor had been converted into a musalla with a brand-new plush red carpet and beige walls. Sofas and mostly empty bookshelves were arranged against two of the walls. A tiny kitchen was nestled on the far right, next to a narrow flight of stairs trailing up to the second floor.

"Zohra, Ashar," Ayoub Mamou said. "The master bedroom upstairs will be turned into a classroom. We labeled everything last night, so—"

"I know, Papa. I was kinda there." Zohra sighed. "C'mon, Ashar."

Shaheer followed her to the truck. "Act like you're annoyed," Zohra whispered to him outside. "Ashar would be."

Shaheer harrumphed. "That's the first thing he and I have found in common." Shaheer thought Zohra smiled to herself at that, but then they became busy with lugging chair after foldable chair to the second floor, followed by used desks of all shapes and sizes. Shaheer couldn't help but feel bad that he wasn't trying harder to talk to his cousin. He needed Zohra if he was going to pull this off. He didn't even know where to begin with Mom. Meanwhile, Ashar the Overachiever had come back with a way to spend even *more* time with Dad. Shaheer needed to try harder to connect with Mom, or he would never be able to convince Dad that he wanted to stay here. He sucked at faking in general.

Zohra broke the ice first while they were heaving a wooden writing desk up the stairs together. "This desk used to be mine and Ashar's," she said, careful not to scrape the already-beaten-up walls. "When we used to share a room. And, you know, before he and Zareena Phuppo moved out."

Shaheer noted the hint of sadness tainting Zohra's words. This was not the same girl who was constantly snipping at Ashar at school.

"You guys used to share a room?" Shaheer asked. They maneuvered the desk into the bedroom-turned-classroom and set it down on the worn carpet.

"Yup. Bunk bed. I always got the top because Ashar's afraid of heights. Our parents finally separated us when Ashar kept leaving his skates around instead of storing them properly and I hit my head after tripping on one of them."

Shaheer winced. "OW."

Zohra laughed like the memory was funnier now than it was painful. "Zareena Phuppo was mad at him for weeks. Ashar felt awful, but he still got booted to down the hall. 'Twas the end of an era. No more sneaking snacks upstairs in the middle of the night and talking way past our bedtime."

Something like jealousy tightened under Shaheer's eyes. He didn't have anything close to a built-in best friend the same age as him growing up. But that didn't explain why Zohra was so grouchy with Ashar *now*.

"Did you know Ashar can eat an entire jar of any spread in one sitting? I'm talking Nutella, peanut butter, jam." Zohra stuck her tongue out in a silent *bleh!*

"So that's what fuels his big mouth," Shaheer mused.

"Right?" Zohra chuckled. "Honestly, if you want to be left alone, just throw a hockey puck as far as you can. He can't resist going after it. Speaking of, I can't believe he dragged you into playing hockey for him! Once he makes up his mind about something, it's over."

Shaheer flopped down on one of the classroom chairs, tired from all the up-and-down. "At least he knows how to get what he wants. I wish some of that confidence would rub off on me. Maybe I could actually stand up to my dad for once about how much I hate that he constantly moves us around." *Whoa*, did he just admit that out loud?

Zohra looked down at her feet, then back up at Shaheer solemnly. "Do you think your guys' plan will work? Bring the family back together by switching places?"

Shaheer hesitated to answer since Ashar wasn't too happy that he'd shared details with Zohra the last time, but Shaheer had just had his butt kicked on ice for the guy. Ashar could deal. Besides, it had been ages since he'd talked openly to a friend. "I want to get to know Mom. If my dad sees how much I want her in my life, too, he might finally stop relocating us. He has to," Shaheer added more to himself.

"Just your mom? What about Ashar?" Zohra asked.

"I don't know," Shaheer confessed. "We're so . . . different."

"Ashar's not all that bad. He just has a problem with, uh, rushed tendencies," said Zohra.

Shaheer raised an eyebrow at her. "Why are you defending him? You always look seconds away from socking him in the face."

Zohra's mouth parted and she looked down sheepishly. "That's not it." Shaheer didn't peg Zohra for the nervous type, so he steeled himself while she contemplated.

"They moved out," she finally said. "Ashar and Zareena Phuppo." Shaheer waited, sensing there was more. "Ashar acted like he didn't want to live with us anymore! As if he didn't *like* it. I never got why they wanted their own house. Our house *is* their house. Why do they need two? I feel like he doesn't care about us anymore. It's so quiet without Ashar and Zareena Phuppo and I hate it." Zohra crossed her arms, all crabby. Shaheer realized in that moment how alike he and Zohra were, bottling up their feelings until they were ready to burst.

"They haven't even come over to stay one night since

leaving." Zohra sniffled and straightened her glasses. "Sorry, I don't mean to dump this on you."

"No, it's okay," Shaheer said. "I get it." Boy, did he. Ashar had no idea how good he had it. "Ashar'll come around. Maybe a good whack in the head with a hockey stick will wake him up."

That earned him a smile. "Thanks for listening, Shaheer," Zohra said. "We should head down. And let me know if you ever, you know, need anything." Shaheer returned the grin, but his insides twisted. Zohra was gonna hate him if she found out that he was just using Mom.

On the main floor, other volunteers had shown up. A few grown-ups and kids, including—

Shaheer halted when he saw two familiar faces, and Zohra crashed into him from behind.

"Hey, Ash!" Ramiz exclaimed. Sohaib's eyes flitted up from his phone and landed on Shaheer. He didn't look happy to see him and Shaheer figured he was still mad about how he'd botched practice today.

"What are you guys doing here?" asked Shaheer.

Sohaib grunted. "I was dragged here."

"You mean you are doing a good deed," one of the uncles corrected him. "When you contribute your time or money to opening a masjid, you accumulate hasanat for it as long as the masjid remains open. Even in your grave after you die!"

"'Kay, Abu. You're the imam. We get it," said Sohaib.

Dada had told Shaheer the same thing. How even a small act of charity would come back to you in your time of need. Opening a masjid was no small task, though. It was a lot of work. Shaheer looked around at the small group of people who'd come today. Even if the plan didn't work out and Shaheer ended up leaving Virginia, at least he knew he'd been a part of something greater than himself. For once.

Shaheer was so far in his head that he didn't think to stop himself when one of the volunteers tried fitting a shoe rack in the foyer. "Don't put that there! You want people tracking mud inside?"

"I don't think anyone will notice," Sohaib said under his breath.

Shaheer ignored him—and Zohra's sneaky kicks to his heel. "Put it outside. That bench, too. It clashes with the carpet."

"Since when do you know about interior designing?" Mom asked in a bewildered tone as Shaheer went over to dig through the pile of donations. There were bookshelves, a water dispenser, a coatrack, cushions, an old sound system, a fan, and boxes of Qur'ans and prayer rugs, among other things. Shaheer's mind filled with ideas. He couldn't do anything about the tragic exterior, but inside . . .

A flurry of excitement passed through Shaheer's chest. He padded over to the kitchen to focus on the house's lay-out from the best vantage point, his mind whirring. What would Jonathan and Drew do?

"Start over," Shaheer said.

Mom and several others blinked at him as if they'd heard wrong. "What?" asked Mom.

"You guys are doing it all wrong," Shaheer explained. "Sofas in the prayer area? Do you want people napping during jummah? And I know bookshelves have a cool aesthetic, but they don't belong in here. Turn one of the bedrooms upstairs into a study. There's space for every-thing. We just have to find it."

Everybody gawked at him like he'd just spoken a dif-ferent language. Instinctively, Shaheer turned to Mom to hear what she thought. She was staring at him too closely for it to be normal, eyebrows bent in his direction, but Shaheer kept waiting. And waiting. This surprised him. He wanted her approval. Where did all of his anger toward Mom go today?

Finally, a smile played across Mom's lips. "What do you think we should do, then?"

Shaheer's heart leaped. "I can show you. Anyone got a pen and paper?" One of the volunteers offered him their tablet, and Shaheer used the stylus to draw a rough diagram on the screen while the others gathered around him. He wasn't the best artist, but his vision got everyone all excited.

"I never would've thought to use a coatrack to hang scarves and tasbeehs. That's smart," an elderly women lauded him.

"Why can't you come up with this kind of stuff at home? It needs a serious makeover—OW!" Ayoub Mamou rubbed his elbow where Mom had pinched him.

"This would really help with making sure we aren't wasting things that can be put to good use," Sohaib's dad, Imam Khalid, commented. "Can someone put the word out on Facebook that we need more hands? Our strength lies in our numbers. We'd like to begin operations in early November. Do you think that's enough time to get this place set up?" Shaheer's chest expanded with pride when Imam Khalid looked to him for approval. He felt like a leader.

"That's plenty of time," Shaheer said. Then, as an after-thought, he added, "In shaa Allah." Shaheer chanced a look at Mom again. No light could match the brilliance of Mom's smile at him, or the tingly warmth traveling down to his toes.

Shaheer and Imam Khalid gave a couple of pointers to get them started. Then everyone rolled up their sleeves and got to work.

Ramiz punched the air. "Gooo, team!"

"Stop it," Sohaib complained. "How is this fun to you?"

"*I* think it's fun. Don't be such a downer," Zohra spat at him. "Have some respect." She patted Shaheer on the back on her way to check out the situation in the kitchen. Shaheer grinned. Zohra was all right.

"Oh, wow! I can already feel the difference," Mom said after a half hour of rearranging. She took in the airier room. "Imagine how much brighter it'll be once we get some nice light fixtures in here."

"Chandelier!" Shaheer said a little too eagerly. "I mean, all the nice masjids have fancy chandeliers." Right? He swore they did.

While Shaheer racked his brain, Mom bent down and dropped a kiss on his forehead. In that moment, Shaheer didn't care that he should've made a stink about being babied in public, or that Mom didn't even know the real him. He thought he might float away on the world's fluffiest cloud.

"There's something different about you, Ash. I can't put my finger on it. But I like it," said Mom.

Shaheer laughed nervously and tried to change the subject, but Imam Khalid beat him to it. "Asr time! Who's giving the adhan?"

"Ashar, obviously," Sohaib said.

Bro, WHAT? Ashar knew how to give the *call to prayer?*

"Ashar?" Mom said after a moment of Shaheer just standing there like a deer in the headlights. "What are you waiting for?" The masjid had gone eerily silent. Every single person was looking at him expectantly. Shaheer heard the adhan every single day on Dada's phone. But he didn't have it *memorized.* Shaheer couldn't even get his *kh* and *gh* sounds right! He wasn't gonna sound anything like Ashar, whose Arabic pronunciation was no doubt flawless.

Shaheer wanted to come out of his skin from the weight of everyone's gaze. He and Mom had just had a moment and now it was going to be ruined. They were all going to find out he wasn't Ashar. From Zohra's pale face across the room, he was sure she didn't know how to swoop to his rescue either.

Ashar's warning about Mom's mood swings nowadays rang in Shaheer's ears. *What if she explodes on me in front of everyone?* Should he fake a sore throat? A stroke? Shaheer's armpits started to sweat, and panic buzzed in his ears. Seconds ticked by slowly as a sense of doom stole his breath.

Then a melodic voice filled the room.

It was Ramiz.

He had his hands up next to his ears and his eyes were closed, the adhan flowing from somewhere deep in his throat. The sound echoed off the walls and bounced against Shaheer's eardrums, wrapping around his shoulders like a warm blanket. Shaheer's heart rate slowed, knowing he was off the hook.

When Ramiz was done, he shrugged casually. "Can't let Ashar steal all the thunder. Besides, he did enough for one day." He winked at Shaheer with a boyish grin that made dimples form in his cheeks.

Something pricked the backs of Shaheer's eyes. Zohra was family, but Ramiz . . . was a brother who had gotten him out of a tight spot. For all his funniness, maybe

Ramiz paid more attention than he gave him credit for. Maybe he had noticed something off about "Ashar" and that's why he'd stepped in. Or he still had no idea and he thought he'd helped his real friend after what Shaheer had told him in the locker room, but it didn't matter. Ramiz had done Shaheer a solid today. He wouldn't forget it.

As they made wudu and lined up for congregation shoulder to shoulder, Shaheer tried to remember the last time he'd felt this way.

Like he belonged somewhere. Like he'd found his people, even if it was in the most unexpected place.

18
ASHAR

Ashar never thought he'd have to be sneaky to pray, but there he was with his forehead touching the ground in Shaheer's walk-in closet. His go-to excuse for disappearing was that he needed to use the bathroom. Dad and Dada were probably starting to think Shaheer had contracted a serious case of diarrhea. Ashar snuck out of the closet, which was conveniently connected to the bathroom, and flushed and washed his hands to complete the ruse.

"All set, sport?" Dad asked when Ashar reemerged in the living room. Instead of the table, they'd spread out books and packets to work on the floor. Dad had suggested they go through a couple of topics Ashar said intimidated him. Dad broke it all down for him into digestible pieces. Ashar wasn't headed for first place at the science fair by any means, but he felt more confident about the Arlington exam than he had before. He was still in the running and wouldn't count himself out until he was *out* out.

"Yup. Let's keep going," Ashar said, eager to take advantage of every minute.

"I think we've covered enough for one day, don't you think?" said Dad. "I don't know about you, but I'm burned out."

Ashar remembered it was his day off and instantly felt bad. It was already past noon. Dad had spent most of their first Sunday together last week catching up on data entry from home, which didn't leave much room to squeeze in fun time.

"Okay. What do you want to do next?" Ashar asked.

"Go for an outing," Dada suggested from his favorite armchair. He lowered the tablet and paused the drama he was watching. "It's not too hot out today."

"DC!" Ashar bounced on the balls of his feet. "You wanted to go, right, Dad?" Ayoub Mamou had taken him and Zohra to all the museums and attractions plenty of times, but there were always new things to check out.

Dad looked at Ashar thoughtfully. "I don't mind. Abba, you up for it?"

Dada loved his walks, but could he keep it up for that

long in the city? Ashar felt bad for thinking it, but he didn't want Dada to slow them down. At least not much about Dada gave away that he was *old* old except for the gray-white roots starting to grow out of his brown-dyed beard.

Dada lifted his reading glasses and watched Ashar closely. Without even blinking. Ashar squirmed under the laser-like focus, his heart pounding. Finally, Dada said, "I'm going to stay back. You two have fun."

"All right. We can head out after my nap." Dad stood up and stretched his arms over his head. He smoothed Ashar's hair as he headed to his room to lie down, setting an alarm on his phone as he went.

"Why the sudden change of heart?" Dada said when they were alone.

"What do you mean?" asked Ashar.

"You haven't agreed to sightseeing in a while. What's so special about DC?" There was that stare that made Ashar feel like he was being examined under a microscope again. Uneasiness tingled in Ashar's chest. *There's no way Dada can tell I'm not Shaheer. Not a chance.* Okay, Ashar had sounded too excited about the trip, but it wasn't like Dada could connect that one little slipup to *definitely* not being *Shaheer*. Shaheer had reminded Ashar on several occasions that he needed to tone it down or Dad and Dada were going to suspect something was up. Ashar insisted he was merely injecting some fun into Shaheer's personality, which Shaheer responded to by flicking an eraser in Ashar's face in study hall.

Ashar shrugged, carefully controlling every cell in his body when he said, "Thought I'd go for a change. The same old is getting boring."

Dada's eyes saddened. "I understand," he said in Urdu. "You must get annoyed with having just an old man for a companion. I'm sorry, beta."

Ashar's stomach twinged with remorse. "I didn't mean it like that, Dada," he said. "You're great. I like spending time with you."

"I know how you must feel. I haven't gone to the masjid around here yet," said Dada. "I don't want to get attached again."

Ashar glued his eyes to the floor at that, as it reminded him of Shaheer. Mom had involved Shaheer in one of her "required" community projects, this time restoring an old house into a masjid. Shaheer liked to emphasize that he was doing it against his will—probably because it gave him another reason to take a jab at Ashar—but Ashar figured out quickly that Shaheer was oddly enjoying it. Ashar occasionally caught Shaheer googling pictures of masjids, and he'd seen things like "Top 10 Interior Design Tricks" in his phone's search history. Ashar had to admit seeing Shaheer so into it was adorable.

Ashar imagined praying in the new masjid with Dada and not having to creep around the house like a burglar. He envisioned Ramadan and Eid with Shaheer, Dad, Dada, Mom, Ayoub Mamou, and Zohra. Eating, laughing, opening gifts, the hugging and chorus of *Eid Mubaraks!* Mom would force Shaheer to wear shalwar kameez and he'd scowl in every picture while Ashar secretly poked him. His whole family, the way it should be. The vision sent a bolt of longing through him, and Ashar wondered when he would get to see his whole family together. But right now, the focus was on spending time with Dad and figuring out why Mom had gone back on her "family first" philosophy.

"You should still go," Ashar told Dada.

A ghost of a smile flickered across Dada's face. "Just as you should make the most of today's excursion. It's nice seeing the two of you spend time together after so long. Now, go and enjoy yourselves." Dada leaned his head back and closed his eyes, the tablet facedown in his lap. "Bring me back a souvenir."

✦ ✦ ✦

"Where to, sport?" Dad asked, surveying the brochure he'd picked up at the station as they sped toward DC on the Metro. They'd dressed comfortably for the occasion. Dad cleaned up well. Ashar decided as he stared at the side of Dad's face that he wouldn't mind looking like that in twenty-some years. Ashar tapped the toes of Shaheer's shoes together, butterflies pirouetting in his stomach from just sitting next to Dad on a train gently rumbling to nowhere and anywhere.

Ashar put his hand over Dad's and tilted the pamphlet in his direction. There wasn't anything on the list he *hadn't* seen, but there was one place he'd go back to again and again if given the choice. "The National Museum of Natural History looks interesting," he said breezily.

Dad chuckled. "You sure are into science nowadays. I don't even have to encourage it."

"It's called the Museum of Natural *History*," Ashar said defensively.

"Yeah, yeah. Excuses." But he folded the brochure into a square and tucked it into his pocket anyway. They got off at the National Mall and walked to the Smithsonian under a clear sky. Even for a late Sunday afternoon, people speckled the green grass and sidewalks underneath the Washington Monument on bikes and picnic blankets.

"How far do you work from here?" Ashar asked Dad as they climbed the museum's steps.

"Not too far. I can show you after this," Dad replied as they were ushered through security. The museum's ginormous African elephant greeted them in the rotunda.

"Take a picture!" Ashar threw his arms and one leg up in the air in front of the elephant's base. Dad laughed and snapped it on his phone. He turned in a circle to observe the signs to various exhibits. "What do you want to see first?"

"Where it all began," said Ashar, pointing in the direction of Ocean Hall and Human Origins.

For the next hour, they wended through the crowd in the different halls and floors, reading plaques, commenting on fossils and artifacts, watching screens mounted flush on the walls playing out history before their eyes. Dad got hung up on the human evolution displays, spouting facts about primitive medical practices that made Ashar glad he was born in the twenty-first century. After ogling the Hope Diamond, they swung back to the first floor for a bite to eat in the café.

Ashar was browsing the menu behind the counter when he saw them. Two little boys with brown hair chilling side by side in a double stroller parked at a table with two women. Identical twins. A warm glow spread in Ashar's belly. His hand developed a mind of its own and tugged on Dad's sleeve. "Dad. Look." He gestured to the toddler twins. "Aren't they cute?"

Dad went still. His eyes were carefully blank, giving nothing away. When he spoke, his voice was low and quiet. "Yes. Have you decided what you want to order yet?"

The tenderness was replaced by a wave of regret. Ashar pushed back on the fizzing hurt. He didn't want anything to ruin the nice time they were having. *Let it go for now.*

Ashar asked for chips and a pastry while Dad ordered a cheese-and-tomato flatbread with coffee. Dad led them to a table as far from the little boys as possible.

"Thanks for coming out with me, sport," Dad said. "I'm having a lot of fun."

"Yeah, same," said Ashar. "We should do this more often."

Dad tore off a chunk of bread and put it in his mouth.

He swallowed and took a deep breath. "Shaheer. I don't know how or when this happened to us. This distance. I guess I have myself to blame for not giving you much of my time." Dad scratched behind his ear uncomfortably, as though he was trying to find the right words. Clearly, he wasn't used to talking so candidly. Like father, like son. "What I'm trying to say is, we can both do better. These last couple of days I've noticed a change. An improvement. You're reaching out to me again. You have no idea how relieved I am. I've been thinking I well and truly lost you."

Ashar felt a spike of guilt. Dad thought he was bonding with Shaheer.

But maybe this was a good thing. When Dad *did* find out he was Ashar, he would realize he had more in common with him and would want him to stay.

"You don't have to thank me," Ashar said. "You're my dad."

Dad reached across the table and threaded his fingers through Ashar's. "And I always will be. We'll have our highs and lows. From now on, let's try to focus on the highs. Deal?"

Ashar nodded, his throat clogging up. He squeezed Dad's hand in return. "Deal."

19
SHAHEER

"What about this one?"

Shaheer shook his head at the Arabic calligraphy Zohra was screensharing. "It's too much. I can't even read what it says."

"Ugh, you are so picky," Zohra complained, her face reappearing on Shaheer's phone. "At least tell me what you have in mind."

While volunteering at the Leesburg masjid this past Sunday, Shaheer had asked Imam Khalid if there was enough budget for them to paint a mural on one of the walls. It was only the first Tuesday night of October. The grand opening was still a month away, but Shaheer had gotten bored of working on his science paper and texted Zohra to see if she was free to look at designs together. He found himself texting his cousin about the masjid even when he wasn't in Ashar mode. Zohra was probably sick of the subject. In exchange, she vented to Shaheer about band drama. Even though he didn't understand a lot of it, it was entertaining.

"It needs to be perfect," Shaheer emphasized.

"Not helping," Zohra said. "What if we went with something completely new and original? I know someone at school that could probably draw it for us. She's really good. I can ask her."

"Really? Who? Do I know—?"

A knock came at Shaheer's door and Dad walked in still wearing his white coat.

Surprised, Shaheer bolted up in bed, fumbling to save his school-issued laptop before it crashed to the floor and deleted his entire science paper.

"Hey, I just got back. Is that a girl's voice I hear?"

"She's a classmate. We were doing homework. . . . I gotta go now. Bye," Shaheer said to Zohra and quickly ended the call before stashing his phone out of sight. "You're early," Shaheer added to Dad skeptically.

"Light commute," Dad chirped. "Wanna take a break and stop by Giant with me?"

"You wanna do groceries right now?" Shaheer asked.

Dad had stopped asking him to run errands together ages ago. Must be the lingering Ashar effect.

They'd settled on a decent routine. Ashar continued filling Shaheer's shoes on Thursdays after school and Sundays. The rare times that Shaheer did cross paths with Dad, he was much happier than Shaheer had seen him in ages. Dad and Ashar had been back to DC on several occasions over the month. Shaheer got to hear all about their adventures from Ashar at school.

Several times, Shaheer thought about how it would make Dad happy that he was finally putting himself out there, but of course, he couldn't. Ironic that it was religious activity that got him pumped up for the first time in forever.

Shaheer had gotten better at his ruse around Mom, too, thanks to Zohra. Sadly, there was no improvement between Zohra and Ashar, and Shaheer was tired of getting caught in the middle. Shaheer was on Zohra's side, anyway. She had every right to be mad at Ashar. How clueless was he? Shaheer felt bad for Zohra whenever he saw her glance at Ashar at school with hurt eyes.

As for ice hockey—Shaheer was lucky to be alive.

"I have to pick Dada's medicine up from the pharmacy." Shaheer's stomach pinched with worry. "Is he okay?"

"His allergies are pretty bad this year and the generics

aren't cutting it," said Dad. As if on cue, they heard a loud sneeze from the third bedroom followed by sniffling and throat clearing. "Unless you'd rather keep working. I understand."

Shaheer's gaze lazily traced a path from the screen back to Dad half turned now in the doorway. He could say no, but the inviting look on Dad's face reeled him in in the end. He did need to be more Ashar-like during his time with Dad so as not to raise any red flags. And part of Shaheer admitted that he wanted to taste some of the ease that they'd lost over the course of all the years and moves, and that Ashar had managed to bring back to life.

Shaheer set his laptop aside and reached down to pull his socks on. "Let's go."

Dad's fingers drummed the steering wheel as he drove. Shaheer lasted about three minutes before pulling out his phone to cover up the awkwardness. At least with Mom, he'd gotten used to talking about her math students and decorating the masjid. There wasn't a single thing Shaheer could think of wanting to share with Dad, and the heaviness of that realization seeped through him.

Dad flitted his gaze to Shaheer in the passenger seat. "So, I've been meaning to talk to you about something," he said. Shaheer tilted his head to acknowledge he was listening while he scrolled.

"The last few weeks, with you and me spending more time together and all, it got me thinking. This whole ER life has me exhausted. The on calls and long hours. I've been wanting to make a switch to something less demanding and I think I've found a solution."

Shaheer's attention snapped to Dad. He was all ears now and not in a good way. "What kind of solution?" he asked hesitantly.

"A more permanent one," Dad said, smiling. "Someone in my professional network reached out to ask if I would be interested in being an investigator on a clinical trial. Big study. A government-funded contract that could last at least three years. There will be other investigators on the project, which means more room in the schedule for time off. Less pay, but I think the trade-off for flexibility is worth it. I'm interviewing next week. If I get the job—which there's a high chance of because I have all the qualifications they're seeking—I wouldn't have to start until December. I know it's soon, but I've heard great things about St. Louis—"

"St. Louis?" Shaheer squawked. "Where is that?"

"Missouri," said Dad.

Shaheer recoiled like something had chomped his insides, and he gripped the door handle to keep from fainting. *Missouri?* They couldn't go there! Why was Dad even telling him this like it was up for debate? *Of course* he would get the job. *Of course* they would move again. Except this time, it was infinitely worse.

Wait. Was it? Dad said it was a three-year contract. If it was guaranteed that they would live in Missouri for a longer time, there was a chance he could finally get his Forever Home over there. So then why was he taking the news so hard?

With a start, he realized it was because Mom and Ashar and Zohra weren't in Missouri. They were *here*. And Shaheer couldn't figure out when that had started to matter to him.

What was he supposed to do? Shaheer had barely spent enough time with Mom for the two of them to gel. One month was nothing, and Dad wasn't going to believe Shaheer if he told him he wanted to stay near her.

"Hey, sport," Dad said after he parked in the grocery store lot while Shaheer internally reeled. "I'm doing this for you. For us. St. Louis would be a fresh start for all three of us. Once my schedule smooths out, I'm thinking of getting reaffiliated with a masjid, too. I grew up in a big, active community in New Jersey, and I'm starting to miss it."

But no other masjid would be the one that Shaheer had spent weeks helping to put together! The one here in Virginia . . . that was *his* masjid. His community. And Shaheer didn't want to let them go.

But he would have to. There was no question. Dad had already made up his mind. If he got the job, they were out. Didn't he know better than to hope for a different outcome when it came to Dad? If Ashar were in Shaheer's place right now, he would've given Dad a piece of his mind. But Shaheer wasn't like his brother. He wasn't this all-around social star who could seamlessly enter someone else's life and repair their damaged relationships. Heck, if he was any good at it, Ashar and Zohra would've made up by now!

It was *so* unfair. He was never going to catch a break.

Shaheer wandered mindlessly around the magazine, book, and candy aisle while Dad waited for Dada's prescription to be filled. He was glad it was a Tuesday evening, so the grocery store wasn't packed and no one could see his hands quiver as he picked up a copy of a magazine and flipped through its pages. That was when he heard something that crushed his lungs in an iron grip and cut off his air.

"Mom, can you please hurry up? I stink. Need a shower bad."

"Just wait, Ash. This'll only take a few minutes."

Shaheer dropped the magazine on his shoes, tiny fires sparking a trail up his arms. *You have got to be kidding me.*

Ashar's groan sounded exaggeratedly through gaps in the shelves as Shaheer frantically picked up the magazine, buried his face behind it, and slunk over to the next aisle. He slowly dipped to the side to peep down the lane. Mom was turned around, one elbow resting on the cart she was pushing and reading the label on a can. The back of Ashar's neck was damp with sweat, and Shaheer realized they'd been on their way home from practice when they stopped. Careful not to tip Mom off, Shaheer grabbed a fistful of Ashar's jersey from behind, covered his scream with a hand over his mouth, and yanked him into the cosmetics section before Dad happened to glance down the aisle and notice them.

Shaheer let him go and Ashar backed into a lipstick display upon seeing him, mouth hanging agape. *"What are you doing here?"*

"Not so loud!" Even their whispered voices sounded like they were shouting.

Ashar cast around like he was looking for somewhere to hide. "Please don't tell me—"

"Dad's here," Shaheer said, confirming their worst nightmare. Ashar shot him a look of pure despair. Shaheer could tell they were thinking the same thing. Mom and Dad absolutely could not run into each other here. It would be chaos. They wouldn't even get a chance to explain, and after the bomb Dad had just dropped on Shaheer, there was no way he was going to risk having his heart torn to shreds by having the two sides of his family meet again without a proper planned reunion. If Shaheer was going to end up leaving, it was better that he and Ashar pretended like none of this had ever happened.

"Where is he?" asked Ashar.

"At the pharmacy."

"Down that way. Okay, good. Maybe they won't—"

"Ash?" Mom's voice carried across the store. "Where'd you go?"

They stood perfectly still. Then Ashar's phone went off, the tinny ringtone blaring through the quietness like crashing cymbals. "Turn it off, turn it off!" Shaheer jogged in place as Ashar's eyes widened in panic.

"It's her!" Ashar said, holding out his phone like it was going to bite him.

The metal noise of a rolling shopping cart turning into their aisle almost gave Shaheer a heart attack, but it was just a woman and her small child stopping to look at toothpaste.

"Ashar." Irritation laced Mom's words now, but at least she sounded farther away in the opposite direction of where they were hiding. "This isn't funny. Get back here right now."

Shaheer didn't think it could get any worse until he heard Dad ask, "Shaheer? Where are you, sport? I got Dada's meds."

"Get rid of him! Don't let him near checkout until we're gone!" Ashar shoved Shaheer in Dad's direction and ducked his head before running the other way.

Shaheer vaulted out of the aisle like the place was on fire and intercepted Dad strolling his way with a white paper bag in his hand. "Dad, we can't leave yet. Um, I just remembered. We need to buy . . . yogurt."

Dad stopped. "Yogurt?"

"For my breakfast. Sometimes I don't have time to wait for Dada in the morning so there needs to be a grab-and-go option. You don't want me to starve until lunch, do you?"

"Of course not, but—"

"Dad, keep your voice down! You'll wake the fish."

"But they're dead—?"

Shaheer pushed Dad by the lower back to the refrigerated end of the grocery store where they kept the dairy products, his stomach tightening with anxiety that Mom would decide to make a detour. Shaheer spun his head every which way, expecting her to appear out of the blue and catch them at any moment.

"I didn't know you liked yogurt," Dad mused, examining the different brands. "Stuff's good for you, though. High in calcium, protein."

"Uh-huh." Shaheer was only half listening, as he was too busy trying to tap into the mystical twin telepathy that would allow him to communicate with Ashar more discreetly. He was still waiting for the part where being a twin was cool. So far, it only gave him a headache.

"Do you want the Greek cup variety? Or the drinkable ones?" Dad asked.

"Strawberry," Shaheer said distractedly. Dad looked at him oddly. "I don't care what kind," he clarified. "Here, let's get these four-packs in different flavors. Keep things interesting."

"Keep things—you really need to get out more," Dad noted jokingly, but stacked a couple of small cups in his arms anyway.

Shaheer's phone hummed, and he breathed a huge sigh of relief when he read the text.

Ashar: Leaving. We just got in the car.
Shaheer: That was close!

It really was a wonder they hadn't accidentally crossed paths yet. Good thing Dad worked in the city and Dada didn't go out much except for walks in their own neighborhood. Shaheer sighed. He needed to break the news to Ashar. He'd rather eat slime.

Shaheer: FaceTime me when you get home?
Ashar: K

"Who're you texting?" Dad asked at the self-checkout.

"Just someone asking about the group project," Shaheer lied smoothly. He and Ashar continued to feed Mom and Dad that story to initiate their Sunday swaps. So far, it had stuck.

"Nice. Maybe you guys can change up your meetup place to 'keep things interesting.'" Dad bagged and tied the yogurt with a snort of laughter.

Shaheer rolled his eyes and put his headphones in

after that. He kept them in the whole ride home and went to deliver the allergy medicine and a glass of water to Dada himself. Then he dashed back to his room, locking the door behind him before climbing under the covers. Ready? he messaged Ashar. A few seconds later, Shaheer got the thumbs-up emoji.

"Why is it so dark on your end?" Ashar asked when he picked up. His face took up almost the entire screen.

"I'm hiding under my blanket. Are you in the *bathroom*?" Shaheer said.

"I'm sitting on the toilet. Don't worry, I'm not using it. Mom's mad at me for ditching her at the store. She kept going on about how I'm never supposed to leave her side when we're out in public. What am I? *Five?*" he said exasperatedly.

Shaheer lifted the covers to make sure the door was still locked before saying in a low voice, "Ashar. We need to talk."

"We are talking."

"Listen!" Shaheer said irritably. "Dad wants to move us again. To Missouri."

Ashar made a choking sound. *"What?"* he screeched. "Tell me this is a prank!"

"I would never joke about this," said Shaheer. "He's interviewing for a position in St. Louis next week."

Ashar sat up straighter on the phone screen. "Just interviewing? That means there's a chance he might not get it," he said hopefully.

"Uh, yeah he will. He always gets the job, and when he does, we'll be gone by winter break."

Ashar paused, resting a fist on his cheek. "Well, you told him you don't want to go, right?"

"What makes you think I have a say?" There was no way Shaheer could give Dad a legitimate reason for wanting to stay without revealing the real reason why.

Ashar sighed. "You're impossible. You know what? Let me handle this. I'll talk Dad out of it. Even if I have to tell him the truth."

Shaheer shook his head. "No."

"Why not?" Ashar asked impatiently.

"Because—" Shaheer said with a tremor in his voice. How could he explain to Ashar that accepting his fate was easier to save himself the devastation of losing yet another potential home? It was the *maybe* hanging over his head like a sword. Maybe Dad would listen. Maybe they wouldn't move. But Shaheer couldn't deal with any more maybes. Ashar's life wasn't one long continuous blur with nothing anchoring him, but Shaheer's was. When you already had a poor track record of anything in your life sticking, you lost faith in the possibility of anything working out in your favor.

And this time was different. If Dad was that willing to patch things up with him, then Shaheer had a better chance of repairing his relationship with the parent he *already* had instead of holding out hope that the other might want to become a more permanent fixture in his life. Besides, Mom had let him go once. Who was to say she wouldn't do it again?

Mom, Ashar, Zohra. Shaheer might never see them again. But the family he already knew, the one that had kept him despite their flaws—they already belonged to him.

"We're not switching places anymore," Shaheer said. "I'm done."

"Are you serious?" said Ashar. "You're giving up that easily? What was the point of us doing all this? What about me? Dad and Dada are my family, too! I want them in my life. I thought you didn't want Dad to move because you wanted to be near us?"

"Well, you had the wrong idea!"

"Whoa, okay. Let's think about this for a sec," Ashar said, offense tingeing his tone. Wow, he must be desperate to want to *think* for once. "You just need a break.

Maybe we can take a week off from swapping places and not worry about it."

Shaheer took a deep, slow breath. "No," he repeated, his voice hard.

"What the heck, Shaheer?" Ashar stammered. "You wanna be the one to go and break up our family *again*—?"

That did it.

"Oh, like you care about family?" Shaheer lashed out. "You still act like you have no idea why Zohra's mad at you and refuse to believe it's your fault! Use your freaking *brain*, Ashar!"

That finally appeared to strike a chord because Ashar fell into a stunned silence. "Wait, what did Zohra tell you—?"

"And I swear, if you do anything to pressure me back into switching, you can forget that you have a brother. I'll never talk to you again."

Shaheer let the strong "drop it" vibe in his words hang in the air for a couple of seconds before ending the video call as forcefully as if he were slamming the door in Ashar's face.

20
ASHAR

Shaheer was a no-show at school the next day. Ashar's heart fell the day after when Shaheer didn't show up for study hall either. He called and texted Shaheer until his fingers hurt, but no dice. It was Thursday, one of their switch days, but it didn't take a genius to know that it wasn't happening. That meant one less day of studying for the Arlington exam, which was fast approaching. But the other half of Ashar's mind wrestled with a completely different emotion while his study hall class worked silently around him in the auditorium: worry for Shaheer.

Shaheer's expression from their last video call was stapled to the backs of Ashar's eyelids. Snippets of his last words to him looped continuously in Ashar's head, but the bit about forgetting that he had a brother was the part that really haunted his sleep. In what universe could he forget something like that? Was Ashar supposed to live the rest of his life not knowing why Mom had neglected her other son? You pretended like you never saw the answer key to a test sitting out on a teacher's desk, not the existence of your twin brother!

Not able to concentrate, Ashar abandoned his geometry homework and put his head in his hands. Ashar couldn't help the sliver of annoyance he felt at Dad for springing this on them. His eyes kept sliding to Shaheer's empty chair a few seats down. Where was he? Was he okay? He'd obviously taken Dad's news hard—too hard. Ashar was sure they could come up with a solution if they worked together. If Ashar could just find Shaheer, he could persuade him to get back to the plan. But short of his urge to kick down the door at Dad's place, Ashar didn't know how, or who, to ask for help.

Well . . . maybe there *was* someone who might be able to help him.

It rankled Ashar to have to swallow his pride, but it wasn't like he had a better alternative. No one else knew about his family's drama. And even though Zohra confiding in Shaheer instead of him upset Ashar more than he cared to admit, at least he knew that meant Zohra was the only other person in the world who cared about Shaheer enough to want him to stay.

Ashar only hoped Zohra would hear him out.

✦ ✦ ✦

When the lunch bell rang, Ashar sped to the cafeteria in search of Zohra. It took him a minute to find her at one of the long tables dominated by the band kids. Zohra was in the middle of listening to one of her friends rant about how the clarinets kept messing up their section of a big piece for their upcoming winter concert when Ashar went up and tapped his cousin on the shoulder.

"I need to talk to you," Ashar said shortly.

Zohra frowned over her shoulder. "Can it wait?" she asked, like he was inconveniencing her.

"No. Now. Excuse us. Family emergency," Ashar said to her friends, and he hauled Zohra by the arm to sit with him at the very end of the table alone.

"What emergency?" Zohra inquired with a trace of concern. "Where's Shaheer?"

"You haven't heard from him either?" Ashar said, deflating.

Zohra shook her head. "What's going on?"

Ashar filled her in on what had happened on Tuesday,

from running into Shaheer and Dad at the grocery store to Shaheer aborting the whole mission after hearing about Dad's interview. Zohra listened without interrupting until Ashar ran out of breath.

"I'm not surprised," she said when he was done.

Ashar blinked to make sure he'd heard correctly. "What do you mean?" he asked.

Zohra blew out a disgruntled breath like she couldn't believe he could be so dense. Ashar was starting to regret coming to her. "Duh he backed out," she said. "Put yourself in Shaheer's shoes. If you moved again and again like that, would you fight to stay in a place where you risk being disappointed if things don't work out, or would it be easier to accept the way things are because it hurts less?"

"I would fight," Ashar said without hesitation.

"Then you don't know Shaheer."

"Right. I forgot you guys are pals now," Ashar countered. "He has a reason to stay here. Mom's here. You and Ayoub Mamou are here. *I'm* here."

Zohra picked the ends of her fading pink hair. "You? What makes you so special?" She didn't sound like she was dissing him, but like she was genuinely curious.

Ashar was baffled. "I'm his brother."

"Means nothing," Zohra said dryly. "All you've done

since meeting Shaheer is treat him like a tool to get what you want. You sprang a surprise switch and a haircut on him by going after him when he wanted to be left alone. You forced him into taking your place at ice hockey so that you could have extra time with your dad. You don't even talk to him about anything beyond this whole brother-swap setup." Zohra bluntly ticked off every strike against Ashar on her hand.

"Hey, I've tried!" Ashar argued. "It's not my fault he prefers to keep to himself."

"Because you haven't been treating him like a brother." Behind her glasses, Zohra's eyes brightened with emotion. "The same way you don't treat me like a sister anymore."

"I never stopped! *You* turned on *me*." Ashar sighed. He and Zohra had never had an argument that had lasted this long, and he was so tired of it. Now that they were holding an actual conversation that didn't involve verbally slapping each other across the face, Ashar just wanted to reach out and wrench the gap between him and his cousin closed.

Zohra crossed her arms and shook her head. "You started it when you moved out of our house without a second thought. You didn't stop to think about how that made me feel at all. It's clear you don't miss living with us."

"What?" Ashar asked, throwing his hands up indignantly. "That's it? That's why you've been mean to me?" Zohra answered by turning to face away from him with a look of betrayal. Ashar kicked her leg under the table. "Zo. Just because me and Mom moved out, it doesn't mean we aren't still family."

"I know that," Zohra snapped. "Doesn't mean I like it. I get that you're like that, Ashar. I know it doesn't mean you don't care about me, that you were just excited about a new beginning, but I always thought us living together was a given."

Ashar mentally shuffled back, recounting the times Zohra had slipped into a noticeably cold silence around him, her biting shots at him. They always transpired around the topic of his and Mom's new place, and she'd been keeping her true feelings from him for weeks. The realization that he'd let her down hit Ashar hard. He acknowledged his mistake the only way he knew how with Zohra. He picked up a plastic spoon off her tray and chucked it at her head. Zohra twisted to glare at him.

"Loser," Ashar chuckled. "Just say you miss me."

A grin wobbled on Zohra's lips. "I don't miss you leaving half-eaten chip bags in my room. At least I don't have to worry about bugs anymore."

"Hey, look at it this way. Now we both have *two* houses," Ashar said.

"Fine. I call the spare bedroom."

And that was that. The tension choking the air between them loosened its grip on their necks and finally let them breathe again. Ashar was relieved things with Zohra were repaired, because that left just one other problem.

"So back to Shaheer," Zohra said, reading Ashar's expression.

Zohra had a point, and Ashar took the time now to analyze everything she'd spelled out for him. Ashar winced thinking about how he'd been an oblivious cousin *and* a lousy brother.

"What do I do?" Ashar asked gloomily.

"Listen, I don't want Shaheer to leave either, but you can't *make* him stand up to his dad. Get him to change his mind the right way by giving him a reason to push back. His desire to stick with us needs to be greater than his fear of losing us. The only way to do that is to show Shaheer that we're there for him no matter what, especially you." Zohra snapped her fingers. "And I think I know just the way to do it. The Fall Fest is next weekend! You should invite Shaheer to go. If we work together to make sure he has a great time, maybe that'll be enough reason for him to want to get back on board with the plan. But it has to be *his* choice."

Ashar perked up. Fall Fest was held in the parking lot behind the town center every year. It *would* be a fun way to take their minds off everything. And since his past methods had been all wrong, Ashar needed the opportunity to show Shaheer that he wasn't as heartless as he'd been making himself out to be this whole time. It might be Ashar's only chance to prove himself to his brother.

"There's just one problem," said Ashar. "I don't know where Shaheer is and he's not responding to any of my texts."

"But he might still reply to mine," Zohra said, whipping out her phone. "Don't worry. Let me handle this."

21
SHAHEER

Dada wasn't having any more of Shaheer's excuses. The I'm-too-sick-to-go-to-school trick would've been more convincing if Shaheer hadn't spent the last two days in bed streaming Disney+.

On Friday morning, Dada told Shaheer neither he nor Dad was going to call the front office to excuse his absence again, so he better get his butt up. Shaheer dragged his feet so that he could at least miss first block to avoid Ashar. Thankfully, Dada didn't scold him for moving at a snail's pace while getting ready. He was probably relieved Shaheer had finally taken a shower.

"I know what you're thinking," Dada said, leaning against the doorjamb while Shaheer combed his wet hair in the bathroom mirror. "But I do think Jawad means well this time. He's trying. I talked to him about it, and this job would be a game changer for us in a lot of ways."

Shaheer sighed. Dad's interview for the Missouri job was in person. He'd wanted Shaheer and Dada to go with him to check out St. Louis together, so he booked them a flight for Wednesday evening two weeks from now.

The last thing Shaheer wanted was to go back to a school he wasn't going to be a student at anymore in a few weeks. To a brother and a cousin and everything else he'd naively allowed himself to think he could have. But Dada would no doubt call the school to make sure Shaheer had reached there and signed in, so *not* going to class was out of the question. Dodging Ashar and Zohra for the rest of the day shouldn't be that difficult, and then he'd have the weekend to come up with a better way to avoid them until December. Shaheer's stomach churned just thinking about having to say goodbye. It was better to cut things loose now while it was still easy for him to let go.

He made it to school right as the five-minute warning bell for second block rang. He went for his locker but halted when he saw Zohra at hers a few feet away. Shaheer was deliberating his escape route when Zohra swung her head to the side and picked him out in the crowd like she sensed him standing there. He quickly ducked and speed walked to science, hoping Zohra had mistaken him for Ashar and wouldn't follow. Shaheer had been ignoring her texts, too, and didn't want to be peppered with questions.

"Shaheer, we missed you on Wednesday," Mrs. Collins said while he was unpacking his books at his table. "We're doing a two-part lab on compounds and mixtures this week. The second part's today, but I still have a make-up station set up if you want to do that first. I suspect it won't take you very long, but you can always come back anytime to finish up part two."

Great idea. Then he could steer clear of Ashar during study hall on Monday. Ugh, was this how Shaheer's brain was going to work for the next two months? Always mining for new ways to hide from his twin until they left town? Harsh.

Mrs. Collins handed Shaheer a blank lab packet while the rest of the class broke up into groups to start on part two. Shaheer went over to the make-up station by himself with his worksheet and pencil. The counter was lined with different substances that he was supposed to identify and write observations about. Shaheer took his time filling out the easy pre-lab questions first and was stealthily reaching for his AirPods in his pocket when a voice startled them out of his hands.

"Hi, Mrs. Collins. Sorry for the last-minute email."

"That's okay, Ashar," said Mrs. Collins. "I don't mind you redoing the lab if it helps you understand the material better. Did you bring a note? Perfect. You can join Shaheer over there. This is a group effort, so feel free to work together."

Shaheer's mood transitioned from unbothered to unamused when Ashar pulled up next to him wearing a wacky grin on his face. "Fancy seeing you here," Ashar said.

"What are you doing?" Shaheer said, agitated. "Why aren't you in—?"

"PE?" Ashar supplied. "They're taking FLE classes. Mom doesn't let me take FLE, so I would've just been sitting in the library. When Zohra told me that she saw you in House A, I had to think fast."

Shaheer's mind whirred and curiosity got the better of him. "You and Zohra are talking again? Wait, Mom doesn't let you take FLE?"

Ashar's smile grew. "Yeah. Zohra and I are cool. And it was all because of you, so thanks!" Ashar slapped Shaheer's arm humorously, but Shaheer just stared at him. Ashar cleared his throat. "Yeah, Mom doesn't let me take FLE. I guess she's a little more traditional."

"Explains a lot about your emotional maturity, actually," said Shaheer, and turned to the items on the counter.

If he was stuck with Ashar for the rest of class, he might as well try and keep them on topic. "Let's get this over with."

"I'm not in the honors class, so I don't have to do the analytical questions at the end." Ashar leaned over to look down at Shaheer's packet with a shudder. "I still don't get the difference between a compound and a mixture."

"It's easy. Here, fill this beaker with water, then add sand and stir." Ashar did as instructed, and they both watched as the sand dispersed throughout the liquid in a muddy suspension. "This is called a heterogenous mixture," Shaheer explained. "Because the sand will settle and separate in the water over time, unlike salt, which dissolves completely."

Ashar scratched his head with his pencil as he mulled it over. "Then what's a compound?" he asked.

"Compounds are chemically combined. They need a reaction to be formed. Like ice. The stuff you skate on is a compound. If it was a mixture, ice hockey wouldn't be a thing," said Shaheer.

Ashar seemed to grasp that, and they did the other experiments so they could write down their observations and classify the resulting substances. Ashar thought too long and hard at some points, and while Shaheer just wanted to move on, he waited and answered more of Ashar's questions.

"You explain things like Dad," Ashar said after a while. "I could've just had you tutor me."

"Well," Shaheer said, rinsing out the last beaker in the sink. "You never asked."

"Really?" Ashar lit up. "You would've?"

Shaheer sighed and dried the beaker with a paper towel before setting it back down. "You didn't come here to redo the lab," he finally said.

"No," Ashar said sheepishly. "Like I said, you were ignoring me, and I didn't know what else to do." There was a pause. "Did Dad do the interview?"

For whatever reason, that made Shaheer laugh. "Not yet. But when he does, he'll ace it. And it wouldn't matter if he did screw it up. He'll try again, and again, and again until he gets a job he wants."

"There has to be *something*—"

"No, Ashar. I told you. There's no point." Shaheer slid his lab assignment toward him and began jotting down answers to the essay questions just to give his hands something to do.

Ashar bit his lower lip like he was physically holding himself back from blathering on and annoying Shaheer. "Well. You know Dad better than me. If you think it isn't worth pushing, then it's not."

Shaheer's pencil froze on his paper and he looked up at Ashar in amazement. "That's it? You didn't come prepared with some grand plan to bully me back into switching places with you?"

"No. I came with an even *better* idea," Ashar said. *Oh boy.* "Have you heard of Fall Fest?"

"Yeah." There were flyers everywhere and Shaheer had heard snatches of conversations as he walked by groups of friends making plans to go together in the hallways. Where was Ashar going with this?

Ashar twirled the front of his T-shirt round and round his finger. "I was wondering if you wanted to go with me and Zohra next weekend. We go every year."

"Me? Go to Fall Fest with you guys?" asked Shaheer, confused. "Why?"

"Because we want you to come," Ashar said earnestly. "*I* want you to come. If there's not a lot of time left before you leave, then we should make the most of it. Who knows when we'll see each other again, or if Mom and Dad will even let us?"

Shaheer bent over the lab to hide his face. He didn't want Ashar to see how his eyes involuntarily fogged up at his words. Ugh, pretending to be Ashar had made him all mushy.

"There are rides, games, food, prizes. You name it.

Next Saturday night. What do you say? Are you in?" Ashar asked hopefully.

A fun outing with Ashar and Zohra. That wasn't exactly a good way to cut loose ends and move on. Ashar was right, though. When would they get this chance again? Could Shaheer pretend like he could start over with a clean slate in Missouri knowing what could've been had he stayed in Virginia? Doubtful, but at least he could leave a part of himself here for Ashar and Zohra to always remember him by. Shaheer hadn't even taken yearbook photos at some of his previous schools. He was just a ghost in most people's memories, drifting from one place to the next in search of peace. He couldn't be a ghost here.

Shaheer didn't have to mull it over for long.

"Cool. I'm there," he said, and Ashar did a happy dance. Embarrassed, Shaheer looked around to make sure no one noticed, but internally, he grinned. Maybe this time, he'd have memories to look back on once he was gone.

22
ASHAR

Fall Fest was the talk of the town. They'd walked out of school the day before and seen a Ferris wheel erected a few roads down. The opening weekend crowd was going to be massive, from what Ashar gathered. He, Shaheer, Zohra, Eddie, and Ramiz planned to get there as early as possible to beat the ticket lines.

"I bet the view from up there is incredible," Shaheer said, pointing at the Ferris wheel from the school parking lot. "Can't wait to find out." Shaheer refused to show it outright, but Ashar could tell he was excited.

"You want to go on that thing?" Ashar asked, trying to mask his anxiety. "You *like* dangling from the air like that?"

"Ashar's a scaredy-cat," Ramiz supplied.

Zohra shoved her glasses to sit more firmly on her nose and crossed her arms over her chest. "He's afraid of heights," she defended him. "Same way you're scared of insects. Would you like it if I shoved a spider in your face?" Ramiz shuffled to stand far away from her.

"We're all meeting up in the town center at six thirty tomorrow, right?" Eddie confirmed.

"Yup. See you then." Zohra and Ashar were going to get ready at her house. Ashar felt bad about leaving Shaheer out, but Zohra's parents were going to drop them off since Mom didn't want them walking to the Fall Fest in the middle of all the traffic.

When Saturday rolled around, they left after Maghrib, the sky plunging from orange to dusk by the time Ayoub Mamou dropped them off near the gates. Now that it was officially fall, the weather was less hot and humid, a breeze struggling to move the air. Eddie and Ramiz caught up to Ashar and Zohra in the line winding around the gravel footpath. Shaheer showed up just as they made it to the ticket counter and Ramiz ragged on him good-naturedly for being late. Eddie and Ramiz were a long way from being Shaheer's close friends, but at least they'd stopped calling him Ashar's "evil twin."

Eddie and Ramiz shot right for the Tilt-A-Whirl.

Zohra's eyes landed on a group of eighth-grade girls taking selfies with big globs of cotton candy. "There's Kelsey," she said. "I'm gonna go say hi. Catch up with you guys in a minute." She exchanged a furtive look with Ashar before leaving him alone with Shaheer.

Ashar suddenly felt awkward. It was wrong to feel like he was on a first date, and yet that was exactly the creepy thought crossing his mind. For a good long while, they walked around in silence, loud music drifting over their heads with the occasional happy scream piercing the air.

"What do you want to do first?" Shaheer finally broke the ice.

"The dragon coaster and Tilt-A-Whirl are always popular," Ashar said, happy to fill the silence. "Oh, and the Scrambler! Don't eat anything before, though. Last year a kid threw up on it." Ashar shuddered. "It went everywhere."

Together, they circled the grounds, showing off their wristbands to the ticket attendants, which allowed them one free turn on every ride. Each stop slowly unknotted Ashar's nerves, especially when Shaheer started filling their time in lines with easy chatter. Ashar took that as a good sign.

Shaheer stopped at the water gun game booth and

pointed to a cluster of neon inflatable swords dangling among the other prizes. "Those are neat."

"Want to have a go?" the attendant—Fred, according to his name tag—asked, gesturing to the row of water guns. "First one to fill their balloons to popping wins."

"Ooooh, I wanna play!" Zohra said, materializing behind them.

Ashar was always up for a healthy dose of competition. They each took a stool, with Ashar sitting between Zohra and Shaheer.

"Prepare to eat dust," Zohra taunted, aiming her gun at the target.

Ashar snorted while lining up his rusty gun with the target. "Fat chance. You're both going down."

"Good luck," Shaheer said sportively.

Fred counted down and waved his hand to signal *Go!* All three of them immediately released thin sprays of water and watched in anticipation as their balloons steadily swelled.

Ashar's fingers curled on his trigger tighter like he could force his gun to spout faster, making his palms sweat. A few seconds later he realized it wasn't sweat—water was leaking from the metal clasp between the gun and the stand. Puzzled, Ashar lost focus, which was a mistake because his shot went wide, spraying the wall behind his target.

"Nice work, Ash," Zohra cackled as she took the lead.

Ashar tried to get a handle on his gun, but the pressure was too much. It tugged sideways and his stream melded with Zohra's, catching her off guard.

"Hey, stay in your lane!"

"It's leaking. I can't get it to—OH MY GOD!" Ashar freaked as his water gun ripped free from its stand with a popping sound. The hose feeding it was still connected to the bottom and he completely lost control of it. Zohra screamed as water sprayed her in the side.

Fred jumped forward, yelling, "Take your finger off the trigger!"

"It's stuck!" Ashar shouted, trying with all his might to swing it around. But that only resulted in him spinning it the other way and shooting Shaheer in the face instead.

"Ashar, STOP!" Shaheer gurgled.

Fred dove for the cabinet underneath the booth and cut off the water. The gun in Ashar's hand went dead. In the ensuing silence, they all sat there stunned, dripping wet. Fred took the defunct gun out of Ashar's still hand. "I guess it's safe to say this one's out of order. Sorry, kids. Um, how about a consolation prize?"

Zohra and Shaheer traded a look over Ashar's shoulder, nodded in agreement, and each took up an inflatable sword to round on Ashar determinedly.

Ashar put his hands up in surrender. "Whoa, guys. You know it was an accident, right?"

"Charge!" Zohra cried, raising her sword over her head. Ashar yelped, running for his life while Zohra and Shaheer chased him around the parking lot, calling him names. He didn't make it far before they caught up and whacked him on all sides.

"Take that!" Shaheer exclaimed, smacking Ashar over the head so that his sword went *squeak!*

Ashar's heart soared despite getting beat up. He soaked up Shaheer's laughter. Where had this Shaheer come from, or had he been here all along and kept himself hidden away?

Once revenge was served, Shaheer helped Ashar up, and the three of them were sitting on a bench near the fence splitting a funnel cake when Eddie and Ramiz found them through the crowd.

"Yo! They have a dunk tank! Guess who was in the seat just now?" Ramiz announced. "Assistant Principal Fowler!" The image of their spindly assistant principal, who oversaw disciplinary action, being sentenced to an appropriate fate was hilarious.

"Shaheer, you wanted to ride the Ferris wheel, right?" Eddie asked, pointing at the enormous multicolored wheel stationed in its own section of the parking lot.

Shaheer slid a look Ashar's way. "Um, it's okay. I'm not that into it." Ashar let out a small smile of appreciation.

"Oh, quit your whining," Eddie said, dragging Ashar up from the bench and shoving him in line with a palm between his shoulders. Ashar's pulse quickened.

"Guys," Shaheer said firmly. "Don't make him if he doesn't want to."

"Who're you gonna ride with, then? It's two people to a cart," said Ramiz. "Zohra doesn't look like she's coming."

One of Zohra's friends had spotted her on the bench and was dragging her away by the wrist to wait in a different ride's line.

Shaheer hesitated, and Ashar chose to plaster on a fake grin even though looking up at the glittering Ferris wheel made him dizzy. "No, it's fine. I'll go with him."

"Ashar—" Shaheer said worriedly.

"Sweet! Shaheer, make sure you get a video of his reaction!"

Ashar's legs shook like Jell-O on a tray as he and Shaheer were loaded into the swinging cart. He tripped on his shoelace and righted himself before he and Shaheer bumped heads.

"You can still get off," said Shaheer.

"Not a chance," Ashar said as the attendant locked them in.

"Why are you so stubborn? You don't have to prove anything to anyone."

"Shut up. I'm reading Ayatul Kursi."

"Oh, for the love of—" Shaheer whispered.

The Ferris wheel gave a groan as it started spinning and all the blood rushed from Ashar's face. His heart pounded in his rib cage as the world slowly shrank beneath them.

"Don't look down," he heard Shaheer say.

Ashar gulped hard, choosing to keep his gaze locked skyward as the ride came to a complete halt about two hundred feet in the air. His hand instinctively shot out to grab Shaheer's as their cart lurched. Ashar's mind kept conjuring all the ways they could plummet to their deaths. Not how he wanted to go.

"Why did you get on if you're this scared?" said Shaheer.

"Because *you* wanted to ride this thing!" Ashar panted.

"I didn't make you!" Shaheer argued.

"I just wanted to do this one nice thing for you, okay?" Ashar spat back, ripping his eyes away from the sky to pin on Shaheer. The bubble of frustration in his chest finally burst. One that had been building since that day in language arts when he and Shaheer first met, inflating a little more each day. "I don't know why our parents lied to us. I don't know why they kept us apart. I don't know why my twin brother doesn't want me in his life badly enough, but I *can* ride a stupid Ferris wheel for you even if it makes me want to crap my pants!"

Shaheer froze, his mouth parting, but no sound coming out. Ashar threw all caution to the wind. They were trapped on this cursed wheel and all he could do to keep his mind off it was to *talk.* "I was so hung up on figuring out what went wrong between Mom and Dad and thinking about my own stuff with ice hockey and the Arlington exam that I didn't stop to think about you. I know you hate me. I'm sorry, Shaheer. I really am." Ashar's voice cracked.

Shaheer's eyes cut away at the apology. Ashar's face drooped. He knew better than to expect more of a reaction from him at this point, but it still stung. Ashar had known Shaheer for—what?—a little over a month, which was no time when you thought about it, but just then, he felt so far from his brother. He *wished* they were close. Ashar had never hated the grown-ups in his life more than he did in that moment. Why had they done this to them? He'd spent weeks trying to come up with a reason that made sense, but nothing did.

The festival noise below them was distant. Up here, it was just the sounds of Ashar scuffling his shoes together and the soft wind mingling with their breaths.

"I don't hate you," Shaheer said, making Ashar jump. "You just don't know what it's like. You think it's cool that I've been to all these places, but trust me, it's not all that it's cracked up to be. I don't have a *life*. You do. You have a home and family nearby, a school and friends you've known for years. You're part of a team and you can set goals for yourself. I never had the chance to do that. At one point I stopped daydreaming that it would happen. Dad just wanted to move up in his career and he didn't care where he had to go to achieve it."

Ashar's heart thudded in his ears. It was like Shaheer had pulled back the curtains in the window of a house he had only ever admired from the sidewalk, whose inside he was finally allowed to tour. To get to know.

"Then this happened," Shaheer went on, gesturing at

the space between them. "And for the first time in forever I thought, this is it. Maybe this is where I'll finally belong. But wanting to stay and being brave enough to stay are two different things. I'm not like you. I chickened out when Dad brought up moving again." Shaheer lapsed into silence. "When I met Mom for the first time, I was so mad at her for leaving me. Do you think you'll ever be able to forgive Mom and Dad for lying to us? Dada, Ayoub Mamou?"

Ashar hung his head. "I don't know. All I know is I don't want things to go back to the way they were before."

The Ferris wheel sprang to life once more, lazily taking them over the peak and around the other side. When they touched ground, Ashar breathed normally again. He jotted a glance at Shaheer. "Do you?"

As soon as the safety bar was lifted, Shaheer descended the platform. He turned on the last step to look back at Ashar's illuminated form standing there, scratching his elbow warily.

"Does it matter what I want?" Shaheer said.

Ashar swallowed the lump in his throat, but before he could respond, another voice beat him to it.

"Yes, it does." Zohra's hand came down on Shaheer's shoulder from behind, squeezing gently. "*You* matter. I know you're scared, Shaheer," she said, reading his eyes. "But you deserve to be happy, too."

Ashar nodded. "You know what would really suck, even more than me not getting into Arlington and getting to play for the Icecaps?" he asked. "Never seeing you again. I don't want you to go."

Shaheer's chin wobbled like hearing that out loud was too much for him to handle. "But Dad's interview—" he said quietly.

"Hasn't happened yet. There's still time," Ashar said. An idea dropped like a location pin in his head, mapping out the fastest route to their destination—revealing their true selves to their parents. It was finally time. The only possible way Shaheer would get to stay in Virginia was if he stood up to Dad. But first, they had to put a stop to him trying to leave.

"What's that look for?" asked Shaheer.

"Uh-oh. That's his up-to-no-good face again," said Zohra.

Ashar grinned mischievously. "Dad can't move you guys if he doesn't get the job."

Shaheer sighed. "We've been over this, Ashar. He always gets the job. Always."

"But what if he didn't this time? What if the interview

ended up being a complete disaster? Or what if—?" Ashar wagged his eyebrows at Shaheer, taking a step closer to him. "He never made it there in the first place?"

It took a minute for Shaheer to catch on. His mouth hung open. "You want to *sabotage* Dad's interview?" he gasped.

23
SHAHEER

Shaheer was an expert traveler. He knew all the steps to get to the gates and all the things that could go wrong along the way. Today, though, it was Shaheer's job to make sure they never made it to the other side of the airport.

Dad's forehead crinkled at the lady holding them up at the baggage counter. He looked like he was ready to break a sweat. They were already running late thanks to Shaheer taking an extra-long shower and "looking everywhere" for his AirPods.

"What do you mean our bags are overweight?" Dad ran an agitated hand across his forehead. "Last I checked, they were well under the limit!"

The airline check-in officer eyed the number blinking on the scale doubtfully. "Well, I'm afraid they all exceed the maximum limit. I'm sorry, but you will have to make some adjustments to get them to fall inside the acceptable weight range."

"I thought they felt heavier than usual when we were loading the car," Dada said at the counter next to Dad. He stroked his chin in a thinking pose.

"Impossible," Dad said. Shaheer was on pins and needles as Dad lugged his, Dada's, and Shaheer's carry-ons off the scale and opened them one by one on the floor. Shaheer scratched the back of his leg with one foot and pretended to stare apologetically at the annoyed passengers in line behind them.

Dad's eyes bulged at the contents of their suitcases. "What's all this?" Dad exclaimed. "Who put all this in here? We're only going for two days. Why did we pack enough clothes for a weeklong getaway? Are we planning on changing our shoes three times a day? Shaheer, why did you bring your school *and* personal laptop? Chargers, headphones—*books*? You don't even own books! Since when do you read?"

"They're school library books," Shaheer said, dead-pan. "I need something to do on the plane." Dada looked at him, a frown digging into his forehead as he silently watched Shaheer gnaw the inside of his cheek. Since

Dad was always on top of their packing, Shaheer had had to sneak in all the extra stuff last minute. If he'd only crammed his own bag, Dad and Dada would've just redistributed the extra weight into theirs. The only way to make sure they got stopped was if all their bags were overweight. So Shaheer piled on whatever he could get his hands on.

It was Ashar's idea, obviously. This whole thing was. Their flight was leaving in one hour. Shaheer had one hour to stall Dad and do whatever it took to make sure they didn't get on that plane. He needed to make sure that Dad missed the interview so that he'd have no real reason to move them away from Virginia.

Then once Shaheer confirmed they'd missed their flight, that was Ashar's cue to bring Mom over to meet them at the airport. But delaying was the easy part. Shaheer dreaded doing what came after the plane left without them. Coming clean to Dad about wanting to stay. For that he needed reinforcement—he needed Ashar. He needed someone who was surer than him—who knew how to get what he wanted. Mom and Ashar were coming one way or another. Ashar made sure of it when he told Mom they were getting a "surprise visit" from one of their New Jersey relatives.

Shaheer's heart thumped. He swiped his fingers over Ashar's last text.

> **Ashar:** Breathe. It'll be fine. You're not in this alone. Dad will listen to you. You're the most important thing in his life. Trust me, I know. Can't believe you haven't figured that out yet

Ashar was completely convinced ruining Dad's interview was the right move, but Shaheer had never felt so tangled up inside.

Even though the outcome of their plan was one big fat unknown variable, Shaheer held on to what Ashar had said to him at Fall Fest. *I don't want you to go.*

Those words—the ones he didn't even know he needed to hear—popped open the spot inside Shaheer where he kept his feelings locked safely away and reminded him what hope felt like.

Shaheer needed to try with Dad for once. To believe as much as Ashar did that Dad would listen to what he wanted because no one was more important to him.

"I don't understand how this happened," Dad groaned,

gesturing at their overspilling bags. "Is there a storage locker we can rent?" Dad asked the lady at the counter. "Perhaps a fee we can pay for the overweight baggage?"

"No, I'm sorry. We don't allow bags over the weight limit," she replied, not sounding all that sympathetic. The next person in line kept checking his watch like he was silently conveying *Get a move on, folks!*

"Can you run back to the car?" asked Dada.

"I'll have to take the shuttle all the way back to the parking garage," Dad said. "There's no way I'll be back in time."

Score!

Shaheer's phone buzzed in his pocket.

Ashar: update?!?
Shaheer: operation a success. so long Missouri ☺

A bubble with three dots appeared on Shaheer's screen but he shoved his phone in his pocket when he heard Dad curse before he could read what Ashar wrote back next.

Dad yanked at his collar with his jaw working. "I can't miss this flight. And I can't reschedule this interview last minute. It was a headache just to find a cover for my shift

212

the next couple of days." Dad scoffed. "Even more reason why I need this job. Forget it. Just throw away whatever you don't need. We'll replace it all later."

They spent the next ten minutes rummaging through their bags. Shaheer dragged his feet, tossing an armload of old shirts, socks, and underwear in the nearest trash bin, and winced, feeling bad. He checked the time. Forty minutes until takeoff.

"Sir," the airline attendant said, tapping her nails on her keyboard. "Your itinerary is only showing two passengers."

Dada shook his head. "We're three."

The woman sighed. "Yes, but only two seats were checked in. One for Jawad Atique and one for Ehsan Atique."

"There should be a Shaheer Atique."

"No one named Shaheer Atique checked in."

"Then do it now!" Dad nearly shouted, his patience fraying.

The lady gave him a disapproving look. "I can't. This flight is overbooked. As of this afternoon, all seats have been claimed by those who checked in on time. Unless someone cancels or misses their flight last minute, this plane is full."

Dad whirled on Dada accusingly. "I thought you checked us in this morning?"

"I don't understand all that online nonsense, so I had Shaheer do it," Dada said, pointing at Shaheer.

Shaheer shrugged, willing his voice not to shake. "I thought I did it right." *Psych.* "Didn't you get the confirmation email, Dad?" he asked innocently.

"I didn't—oh my God. Do I have to do everything around here?" Dad complained.

"Gentlemen, if two of you would still like to take this flight, I can check your bags in and print your boarding passes. But please, I need you to step aside so I can assist other people," the attendant said exasperatedly.

"Shaheer can't stay by himself," Dada said once they collected their belongings and moved out of the line to stand in front a small duty-free shop in the middle of the huge check-in area. A set of wide stairs in the middle of the room led down to international arrivals and transportation.

"I know, Abba," Dad snapped.

"It's okay, Jawad. Mishaps happen," said Dada. "You go on without us. Shaheer and I will head home. If you hurry, you can still make it."

It was now or never.

"Why can't we all just go home?" Shaheer asked before he could second-guess himself.

Dad and Dada stopped in their tracks, temporarily

forgetting they were on a time crunch. "What do you mean?" asked Dad.

"I mean, who cares about Missouri? Why do you need that job anyway?" Shaheer's voice was small, but he forced the words out, even though the way Dad was looking at him made him want to puke. Shaheer was vaguely aware that his phone was vibrating, but he couldn't check right now, or he'd lose his nerve.

"Why can't we just stay here?" Shaheer asked softly.

Dad stared at him like he was trying to solve a tricky riddle written all over his face. "You want to stay here? Why? That makes no sense. There's nothing here for us. In St. Louis—"

"Dad, I don't care what's in Missouri!" said Shaheer. "I'm not you. I don't like moving! What if I just don't want to go?"

Dad's eyebrows pulled together. Dada, on the other hand—Shaheer didn't know how to describe the way his grandfather's soulful gaze dwelled on him.

"Shaheer," Dad said. He sounded irritated. "I don't have time for this right now. We can talk when I get back." He reached for his suitcase's handle. Shaheer surprised them by grabbing hold of it first and tugging it out of reach.

"Shaheer!" Dad reprimanded. "Why are you behaving like this? This is not you."

A pressure built behind Shaheer's chest. What did Dad know? He wasn't even trying to understand him. To listen. Dad didn't *know* him. Heck, he probably knew Ashar better than Shaheer. Suddenly, Shaheer remembered why he'd shut down years ago and let Dad lead him along like a leashed dog. He'd been right all along and Ashar was wrong. Dad wasn't going to choose him. His job—what *he* wanted—was always going to be more important. This just proved it.

"You're the worst," Shaheer said. Dad's suitcase clattered to the floor as Shaheer tossed it aside and half ran toward the stairs. He didn't wait up for Dada. All he wanted was to get away from Dad and never talk to him again. He could stay in Missouri by himself for all Shaheer cared.

"Shaheer!" Dada called out to him.

Shaheer didn't respond. Didn't even look back as his foot hit the top of the staircase.

"Ashar!"

A gasp caught in Shaheer's throat. *No. Did Dada really just call him—?* He flipped around, panic zapping at his brain in full force, but his shoelace jammed itself underneath his foot and threw him backward. Shaheer pinwheeled his arms, trying to regain his balance as he watched Dad and Dada's alarmed expressions tilt downward. Shaheer waited for the impact to his head on the stairs, but a pair of arms rescued him from a trip to the ER.

Shaheer looked up at who'd saved him.

It was Ashar.

"You're here already?" Shaheer cried.

"I sent you, like, a thousand mayday texts!" said Ashar. "Why weren't you reading any of them?"

"Ashar?" The familiar voice sent a current up Shaheer's spine. He felt his stomach drop straight to his feet when Mom, wearing a black peacoat, came into view behind Ashar. Her footsteps faltered when her gaze landed on them. Shaheer gripped Ashar's shoulders as he looked back at Dad and Dada. His heart zinged when he saw them gaping at Ashar. Then it froze all together when Mom halted midstep with a look of complete horror at Dad and Dada.

Shaheer gulped. *Oh, here we go.*

24
ASHAR

"Zareena?" Dad breathed.

"Jawad?" Mom said on a choked breath. She lifted a hand to her mouth. "Is that you? What are you *doing* here?"

Dad's head whipped from Shaheer to Ashar, then back to Shaheer again. When the realization of what was happening set in, Dad turned white as chalk, his mouth wide open in shock.

Ashar hoisted Shaheer upright and wrung his hands. For once, he was speechless. "Uh, surprise?"

Dad slowly backed away from Ashar and Shaheer and nearly tripped over his suitcase. He pointed a shaky finger at their faces. "You two know each other?" he asked in a quivering voice.

"We can explain!" Shaheer said, giving Ashar a tense

you first look. Ashar felt sick. He had no idea what had gone down between Shaheer and Dad before they'd arrived, but the cat was out of the bag now. Where did he start?

At first, nobody moved. It was like they'd all hit pause to let their brains catch up to what they were seeing. Then a smile slowly stretched across Dada's face.

"You know, I'd like to think I know Shaheer very well. When he started acting funny, I got the sense that something unusual was going on," Dada said. "I was right." He came over and knelt in front of them. He reached out and laid a gentle hand against Ashar's face, like Dada needed to make sure he was real. "You rascals. You've been switching places on us, haven't you?"

Ashar went numb all over. "Wait, you knew this whole time?" he asked.

"I had a hunch, but I couldn't be one hundred percent sure. I guess I didn't dare to believe . . ." Tears instantly glimmered in Dada's eyes, and he pressed his forehead to Ashar's. "Subhanallah. 'He is the best of planners.' All I ever prayed for was for my boys to be reunited in this world. And now look!" Dada was crying for real now. He pulled Shaheer and Ashar to his chest tightly.

Ashar fell apart right there. Dada was seeing *him*. Just

for a moment, he forgot about why they were there and pretended like Dada had the power to make everything right. He and Shaheer had been ripped from each other, but Dada's duas held them together through an invisible rope until they finally met again. He and Shaheer would spend the rest of their lives not knowing how to repay him for always thinking about them.

"Abba," Mama said, the word spilling naturally from her mouth even after all these years.

"My dear Zareena. It's so nice to see you. By the way, I had no part in any of this," Dada said innocently. "I'm just as surprised as the two of you."

"But how—?" Mom's gaze went to Shaheer. Shaheer, to his credit, didn't look away or move to hide behind Ashar. Instead, he put one hand on Ashar's shoulder and said, "Hi, Mom."

Mom gasped like she was hearing her baby call her "Mom" for the first time. Which, when you thought about it, was kind of true. "Shaheer," she said, her chin trembling. Ashar had seen Mom upset, stressed, and exhausted, but she always kept it together for him. This was the first time Ashar was seeing Mom's composure shake, like it was taking all her effort to stay standing.

Something about Mom's reaction finally slapped Dad out of his stupor. He stared at Ashar like nothing else in the world mattered. "Ashar."

Dad finally acknowledging him as his real self roused Ashar's voice. "Yeah. It's me."

"Wow, you look—so alike." Dad chuckled, but there was no mistaking the way his eyes were reddening. "Did I hear you've been switching places on us?"

"Yeah, a couple times a week since school started. On Thursdays and Sundays," Ashar said, wiping his nose with the front of his sweatshirt. "The semester-long group project was made up."

"What?" Mom shrieked at the same time Dad exclaimed, "You go to the same school?"

"Yeah, that's where we met and everything just sort of came out," said Shaheer.

Mom clutched her head like she was trying to keep it from rolling right off her shoulders. "I don't understand. How have you been able to keep it a secret until now?"

"Well, we didn't think telling any of you guys the truth would be a good idea," said Ashar. "We were afraid that Dad would make a run for it. Besides, it wasn't a total secret. Zohra knew we were swapping lives this whole time. Remember our trips to the museum?" Ashar asked Dad. "That was me, not Shaheer."

"And *I've* been the one helping out with the new masjid," Shaheer told Mom.

Mom and Dad exchanged a dumbfounded look.

"But why?" Dad asked. "What was the purpose of lying to us this whole time?"

"You mean how you guys have been lying to *us* for years and made everyone else lie to us, too?" Ashar said stiffly. "Did you think you could get away with it forever?"

Their parents shifted uncomfortably, not meeting their gazes.

"You did," Shaheer answered for them. "If we hadn't moved here, we would have never found out."

"But we did, and you know why?" Ashar continued. "Because of Dada. He's been making dua for us ever since you split us up. He's the only person who cared about us."

"That's not true," Mom piped up. "I did care about you. Both of you."

"Then why is this the first time all of us are here?" asked Ashar.

"Ashar," Mom admonished. She swept a hand around the airport. Through the big floor-to-ceiling glass windows, the sky was already dark, streetlights casting the sidewalks outside in a sickly yellow glow. "Not here."

Ashar shook his head and crossed his arms stubbornly. "Yes, *here*. We're not leaving until you talk."

"Young man!" said Mom.

"It's all right, Zareena," Dad said, rubbing the back of his neck like the whole situation was one big inconvenience. "We can't blame them for wanting answers."

Mom whirled on Dad like she'd been waiting to lash out at him. "I realize he's upset, but it doesn't justify talking to us like we're their age."

Dad laughed, the sound cold and sharp. "You raised him."

Mom's eyes narrowed dangerously. "What's that supposed to mean?"

"He must've picked up on it from somewhere. If memory serves, you used to be the same way once upon a time."

Mom's posture was rigid. The tension in the air was drawn out like a rubber band about to snap. "Are you insinuating that I taught my son to be disrespectful?" Mom's voice was getting shrill, making the hairs on the back of Ashar's neck stand on end.

"Oh no," Dad said, holding up his hands in mock surrender. "God forbid I criticize you for anything. Even nicely. I'll never forget how you lost it on me that time I told you I didn't think you were putting in enough effort to spend time with me."

"We had *twins*, Jawad!" Mom was practically screaming now. "*Two* babies! And we were both working crazy hours. Teachers get a lot of work, too. Doctors aren't the only ones who get to hog the 'overworked' title."

"Abba was there!" Dad shot back. "We had family around to help us, but *you* didn't want the help!"

"Well, I'm sorry I was trying my best to be their mother and not drop them in other people's laps!"

Dada sidled closer to Ashar and Shaheer like he could shield them from their parents' harsh words. Ashar shivered like he was cold. Mom and Dad didn't care at all that they were standing right there. That they were truly meeting their sons for the first time in years, yet all they could think about in that moment was pushing each other's buttons.

"If it hadn't been for the settlement agreement, I would've taken Shaheer in a second," Mom said. "I had to lock that pain away for Ashar's sake, but I'll never forget."

"Did it surprise you that I fought to keep them?" Dad said dryly. "They were mine, too."

It was Mom's turn to scoff-laugh. "Barely. You were more concerned about going anywhere and doing anything besides staying home and taking care of them!"

"And you never liked going anywhere or doing *anything else*," Dad complained. "You know what it felt like to be married to you? It was like being trapped."

Ashar's stomach knotted. This was turning ugly. How could they be physically so close together yet so far apart at the same time?

He nudged Shaheer. They could get their parents to come to their senses if they made good on their original plan. Shaheer could get them to stop fighting if he put his foot down and told Dad he didn't want to leave. Now was the time. But Shaheer wasn't saying a single word. He wouldn't even look at Ashar. What was going on?

Despite everything, Mom looked hurt. "Well then, I'm glad you were able to be free of me. Finally got that off your chest after all this time, huh?"

Dad rolled his eyes. "Oh please. Don't play the victim card. You said some pretty nasty things to me in the past. You were always name-calling me and blaming me for the smallest stuff."

Ashar was unable to hear any more of this. The overwhelming urge to defend Mom smothered all his other senses. "Hey, don't talk to her like that! Why do you have to be such a jerk?"

Shaheer spun around to face Ashar and finally broke his silence. "She yelled at him first," he argued. "If anyone's being a jerk, it's Mom."

"Why are you defending him?" Ashar yelled. "Didn't you hear? He barely spent time with us back then. Mom did all the work. He probably only took you because he wanted to take one last dig at her, not because he really wanted to keep you."

"Ashar!" Both their parents and Dada were mortified this time.

Ashar saw Shaheer's hands tremble, and he wished he could take his words back. But words were like arrows. Once you let them go and they hit their target, you couldn't take the arrow back without leaving a hole behind.

"Great boy you raised there, Zareena," Dad said, coming over to put his arms around Shaheer protectively. "Now I don't feel so bad about my parenting."

Ashar's face crumpled like Dad had slapped him. All those days they'd spent studying together, going back and forth about what to order, exploring DC, snickering behind Dada's back when he'd get on their case—gone. Just like that. Maybe all those times had never been real. Maybe *this* was reality. He'd thought some time together would change things. That his parents would see how much they'd missed and admit that separating him and Shaheer had been a mistake. He'd been so wrong. Maybe they never stood a chance. Weeks of trying . . . none of it had mattered.

"How dare you!" Mom yanked Ashar away from Dada and to her side. "I don't have to stand here and listen to you insult him like that! Let's go, Ashar."

"Wait." Ashar wriggled in Mom's grip to face Shaheer, who was staring down at his shoes. "Shaheer."

"I don't think your brother wants to talk to you right now, Ashar," Dad said sternly.

Regret coated Ashar's throat. "Shaheer," he pleaded again. Shaheer refused to look at him. Ashar swallowed bile. This was not the plan. They weren't supposed to fight. They were supposed to be in this together. Ashar couldn't just leave Shaheer now after the awful thing he'd said to him.

But it was no use. Dad put his hand on Shaheer's lower back and pushed him away from them without another word, motioning for Dada to follow. Mom twisted Ashar around in the opposite direction and paraded him back down the stairs to the car, all while Ashar wrestled with the urge to rip his tongue out and chuck it in the trash.

25
SHAHEER

Two weeks went by without a peep in their house.

They hadn't heard from Mom since the fight at the airport, and Dad was perfectly fine with not talking about it. Or talking in general.

Shaheer didn't think the silence could burrow itself in his chest any deeper when it completely split open one Thursday night while he was doing math homework. Dad's and Dada's loud voices almost broke down his door.

"I'm astounded she even agreed to let you take him!" spat Dada.

"You always make me sound like the bad guy!" Dad said in a biting voice. "I know you think I've been a bad parent all these years. But I can't believe you're blaming this whole situation on me!"

Shaheer squeezed his eyes shut and turned up the volume on a new show he was trying out because he couldn't stand to watch the Property Brothers be all *twinny*. His eyes kept drawing to his phone on the pillow next to his laptop. Shaheer had lost count of how many times he'd caught himself staring at the screen these last two weeks, waiting. He'd been so sure Ashar would've apologized to him by now. Shaheer tried to convince himself Ashar was just keeping his distance because he was overwhelmed. The next few days were huge for him—the Arlington exam was on Saturday, and so was the Husky Bladers' game against the Cardinals. He probably didn't have any space left in his brain to think about anything else.

But would it kill Ashar to send him a text? It took, like, ten seconds. Ashar had turned into a completely different person around him. The kind that refused to acknowledge his existence, like he couldn't see Shaheer.

Shaheer tried not to miss Ashar. Didn't want to admit that he missed him most of all. But if Ashar thought Shaheer was going to go to him first, then he had another thing coming. What Ashar had said to him at the airport wouldn't stop spinning in his head like sharp disks. And . . . there was no way Ayoub Mamou didn't know what had happened. Why didn't he or Mom reach out to Shaheer? Zohra was the only one still talking to him, but it wasn't like before. It was like Zohra was scared of Shaheer poofing out of existence if she got too deep.

If none of them wanted anything to do with him, then fine. Whatever. Shaheer couldn't believe he'd started to *care* about these people.

You should've just stuck to being invisible, Shaheer scolded himself. He was back to square one: all by himself in a new town with just his headphones to keep him company. The Forever Home dream was lost. It just wasn't meant to be, and he'd have to live with it.

The whole universe was dunking on him, and Dad and Dada still wouldn't shut up.

"I wanted to tell Shaheer, but I was scared that if he found out the truth, he would hate me. I should never have let you and Zareena get away with it." The catch in Dada's voice was noticeable through the wall, like after all this time, it still pained him. "You let your hatred for each other win out against what was in your sons' best interests. I lost a lot of respect for the two of you after that, but I didn't lose faith in Allah. Ashar is *right here*, and you aren't doing a damn thing about it!"

"What does it matter?" Dad replied. "Legally, he belongs to Zareena."

"What about me?" Shaheer yelled from his bed before he could stop himself. The rage filled him so fast he didn't even notice that he'd jumped out of bed and sped out into the living room to face Dad and Dada head-on. "Do I 'legally belong' to you, too?" he asked, standing right in front of them, his hands balled into shaking fists at his sides. "An object you can selfishly take with you wherever you go? Did you want to keep me, or was Ashar right? Am I just a prize to you?"

Anger and hurt flickered across Dad's face. Shaheer saw whatever headway they'd made in setting things right between them crumble before his eyes.

"I wanted both of you in my life," Dad responded quietly.

"But you left Ashar," said Shaheer. Saying Ashar's name out loud hurt physically. "You left him, and you never looked back, just like you do with everywhere we've lived. And now you want to do it again."

Dad had managed to reschedule his interview remotely. A contract had already arrived in the mail. They would be leaving for Missouri two weeks before his start date in December. It would just be Shaheer, Dad, and Dada again. But this time, nothing would be the same. How were any of them supposed to start over? Shaheer couldn't ignore the years of lies and betrayal that had come to light. Maybe two months ago, Shaheer would've kept his opinions to himself if he knew what was good for him. But Dad let him down hard at the airport. And this time, Shaheer had a reason to push back.

Or so he thought. Guess Ashar didn't feel the same way. He probably couldn't wait to get rid of Shaheer. So then why was Shaheer hoping against all hope that his brother still wanted him around? The only person who ever looked out for him was standing across from him, a riot of emotions swirling on his haggard face. Shaheer didn't care if the distance between him and Dad was so wide it was a three-day journey by boat to cross it. At least he had Dada. The only person in the world Shaheer knew he could count on, who wouldn't leave him.

And that's why he said, "We don't even have to wait until December. I say we ditch this place as soon as possible."

Worry slipped into Dada's voice. "Shaheer—"

"It's okay, Dada." Shaheer didn't want to find out how

it would end if Dada kept pushing Dad to go to Ashar because of Shaheer. But if Shaheer made it clear he wanted nothing to do with Ashar, then it was pointless. Shaheer just wanted Dada, and Dada needed Dad. He couldn't live alone. "Dad's a pro at running away. We'll be outta here in no time. It didn't take long for him to dump Mom and Ashar."

Dad's face clouded over like a storm. A minute passed in silence, but it felt like hours.

"Look, Shaheer," he finally said. "When you go through a hard time with someone, you start to see their true colors. Your mom couldn't have my back, and I couldn't have hers. We'd tested each other's patience repeatedly, and I just couldn't handle any level of interaction with Zareena. Even for your and Ashar's sakes. When things get that bad, you take what you get and move on with your life. Staying together for your kids is not the best option when it means not being able to be the best version of yourself with the other person."

Shaheer couldn't believe Dad was discussing him and Ashar as if their existence were an *agreement*. Like the last slice of pizza he and Mom fought over. They said they cared about him and Ashar, and maybe that was true, but they cared about themselves *more*. Shaheer wasn't even surprised when tears started building in his eyes. He went off like an epic fireworks display, no longer sputtering to spark.

"HOW WAS THAT OUR FAULT?" Shaheer demanded. "Why did Ashar and I have to be punished because you and Mom sucked at being together? None of this would have happened if you guys hadn't split us up!"

Dad's eyes were wide. He looked like he was trying to remember how to breathe.

Shaheer's shoulders rose and fell rapidly. "If you really wanted Ashar in your life like you said, you would've tried. He wanted to get to know you so bad that he pretended to be me so that he could spend time with you. Don't you care about him after all that? He deserved better. *I* deserved better! I deserved a *home*! You raised me my whole life and you still erased me! But it's too late to fix now. Even if you change your mind, I'm not. I don't want to stay here."

Dad didn't answer him. He stared at the wall for a good long while before turning on his heels and walking to his room, shutting the door behind him. It didn't matter where they went. What happened here would follow them like a bad dream, probably forever.

Dada patted and kissed Shaheer on the head, like he was proud of him for speaking up but sad that it had to be this way.

Besides, what was the point of a home if the people who should care about you didn't show up for you?

26
ASHAR

It was late and Ashar should've been in bed. Tomorrow was a big day, but the crushing stress stole any chance of rest. So, there he was haunting the kitchen for a late-night snack even though he wasn't hungry.

Ashar was digging around in the fridge when the lights flipped on unexpectedly. Startled, he bumped his head on the shelf above him as he whirled around to find Mom standing at the foot of the stairs in her pj's.

"What in the world are you doing up so late?" Mom asked. "You have an early start tomorrow."

Didn't he know it. Ashar was supposed to be at the testing center at eight a.m. sharp, then speed right to the icehouse afterward. His hockey bag and stick were already waiting next to the front door. He was going to take the

Arlington entrance exam in his jersey so that he wouldn't have to rush putting his gear on before the game. If he let himself dwell on all the things that could go wrong, Ashar was sure he'd just curl up into a ball and weep. Instead, he said nothing as he went over to the pantry.

"Ash, you've been panicking about this exam since the summer and you're going to let all your hard work go to waste for—" Mom frowned at the jar Ashar reached for on the bottom shelf. "Nutella? That is *not* brain food."

Ashar stayed ignoring her as he spread a thick layer of hazelnut chocolate on a slice of bread. This was the first time since the airport incident that Mom was speaking to him directly, other than the epic lecture he got in the car on the way home. It felt wrong to walk around avoiding Mom and pretending like they didn't know each other. But every time Ashar convinced himself to let up on her, the way she'd jumped down Dad's throat whipped around in his mind like an air hockey puck bouncing off the walls.

Ashar had been afraid this whole time that Shaheer would see Mom's bad side, and he had. But in the end, it was Ashar who revealed how nasty he could truly be. He couldn't stand his own reflection after what he'd said to Shaheer, much less summon the courage to apologize.

On top of that, Ashar spent days being hurt over Dad's initial reaction to meeting him again not being as heart-felt as he'd wanted. Yeah, he'd been too stunned at seeing him and Shaheer together to process anything else, but still. He couldn't even call their reunion "happy." There'd been no tearful hugs or any sort of sappiness. Then it ended in disaster because he couldn't get a handle on himself.

Of all the people he wanted to scream at, Shaheer was never one of them. And now he was too embarrassed to share how he was feeling with the one person he needed most. Just having his brother's calm presence around would've taken some of the edge off. He'd kill to even hear Shaheer tell him to quit being dramatic. Or to go easy on the Nutella.

Ashar took his sandwich and a glass of warm milk over to the dining table. He ate quietly in his pajamas while Mom watched. She looked shaken up at his silence, like she didn't know what to do with this version of him. There was no foot stomping, no raising his voice. He didn't even glare at her. Even though on the inside he felt like a pressure cooker about to pop off, Ashar was the picture of perfect patience as he chewed his food.

"All right. You're freaking me out," Mom said, gripping

the back of the chair across from Ashar. "Say something or I'm gonna have to assume you're really Shaheer." Mom's eyes rounded. *"Are* you Shaheer?"

Ashar lurched at the casual way Mom dropped his name like she hadn't kept Ashar's own twin a secret from him his whole life. Shaheer's question from the Fall Fest flitted back to mind. *Do you think you'll ever be able to forgive Mom and Dad for lying to us?* Did Ashar have it in him to hold that against Mom forever?

"Maybe," Ashar said, not sure if he was answering Mom's question or his own.

Mom peered at him and snorted. "Definitely Ashar."

"How would you even know?" Ashar snapped. "Not like you know him at all to tell the difference. I didn't believe you, by the way. When you said you would've taken Shaheer, too, if Dad hadn't fought you. If you really loved him that much, you wouldn't have left him." *And Dad wouldn't have left me.*

Darn it. Ashar squeezed his sandwich in his hands until chocolate oozed out onto his fingers. Why had it taken them this long to learn there was no getting through their parents' thick skulls?

Mom's face changed. A stillness came over her like

she'd been turned into an ice sculpture. "You wouldn't understand because you're just a kid."

"Oh, I understand," Ashar said. His voice wobbled and his throat was tight, but he refused to give in to the heat rising to his head. He forced himself to stay composed. That was the only way his next words were gonna land. "If you couldn't have both of us, you should've at least tried your hardest to make sure Shaheer and I stayed together. Why couldn't you and Dad set your differences aside for us? I know that people get divorced for a lot of reasons," Ashar blubbered on. "I know that not being in love anymore is real. But that doesn't mean you stop loving *us*! We're both your kids! We belonged together! We shouldn't have had to switch places and pretend to be each other to get you guys to want us and stop being jerks. Even that was a waste of time!"

Ashar was starting to regret coming downstairs.

"You're right," Mom whispered. Ashar thought maybe he'd heard wrong, but then Mom slid the chair out to sit down and said it again. "You're right. What we did was selfish. I always knew that, but seeing how hurt you are—" Mom placed her palms flat on the table and took a trembling breath. Ashar could almost feel her collecting her thoughts, trying to stay calm like he was. Seeing Dad again had seriously damaged her put-togetherness. "You have every right to be mad at me and your dad. But Shaheer didn't deserve the way you treated him."

"You think I don't know that?" Ashar didn't have the guts to face any of them over there. Not even Dada. Ashar desperately wanted to repair the damage he'd done, but he didn't know how.

Mom's face creased with sadness. "You guys really care about each other, don't you?"

"Not sure about Shaheer anymore, honestly," Ashar huffed. He dropped his mangled sandwich on his plate. "I shouldn't even be thinking about this right now. It's distracting."

Mom reached out her hand across the table, then snatched it back like she'd thought better of it. "I've been thinking about it a lot these last few days. Ayoub and I had a long conversation, too. He chewed me out." Mom's eyes shone, which immediately triggered Ashar's own tears to slide down his face. "But everything he said was true. I'm sorry, Ashar. I've always tried to do what's best for you, but I really messed up when it came to your dad and Shaheer. You're right. It was not your or Shaheer's responsibility to come to us. We're the adults. We should've been the ones to come to *you* first, and it should not have taken this long. But I never wanted either of you to see our bad sides, which is why we did what we did. It was the only way we could see forward that was best for all of us. You have to know it was the hardest decision I ever made in my life." Mom closed her eyes, filling the space between them with remorse.

Now Ashar got why so many people had kept silent all these years. Even if the decision to split him and Shaheer up hadn't been any one person's fault, going along with it was everybody's. Everybody who'd been afraid of splintering the family even further. Dad and Dada, maybe even Mom and Ayoub Mamou would've clashed bad enough to never speak to each other again. Their acceptance wasn't really acceptance at all, but a shield to block him and Ashar from even more grief. They were all just trying to stop the hurt from spreading.

The same way Ashar was avoiding Shaheer to keep a handle on himself from doing or saying anything that would make things worse.

"If you give me a chance, I'll do better," Mom said.

"Better?" Ashar hiccuped, his eyes flitting up at her.

"I've never asked Jawad for anything. Not even money. But if I have to swallow my pride and reach out to him to figure out what we can do for you and Shaheer—I'll do it. For you, and for Shaheer. I can't promise that Jawad and I will get along," Mom warned. "But I'll try if that's what you want me to do. And I won't yell at your dad again. On second thought, I can't promise that either."

Ashar laughed, feeling lighter and heavier at the same time. They could fix their broken family, if only a little bit. There was hope. But Mom made it clear it was *his* call. She would do what he asked her to. But sending Mom to clean up his mess was wrong. Ashar needed to be the one to make it right. The thought of losing Shaheer— the fear of that happening took a seat in Ashar's heart and refused to budge. But what was he to do? How could he prove himself to Shaheer? What if nothing Ashar did would ever be good enough? Would he and Shaheer do what their parents did years ago and walk away from each other for good this time?

Mom's fingers brushed Ashar's hair back from his forehead. "We can discuss it more later. Get some rest, kiddo. You're gonna do amazing tomorrow, but you'll need your energy."

Ashar looked at the clock on the microwave and—
oops. He really should hit the sack. After the Arlington
exam, he had to stay alert to kick Cardinal butt and hopefully impress the Icecaps coach. Then he could focus on
getting his brother back.

27
SHAHEER

Zohra texted Shaheer on Saturday while he was taping boxes together in his room, packing away as many of his clothes as possible. He set the masking tape aside and unlocked his phone.

Zohra: Hey, are you going today?

Shaheer's eyebrows squished together. There was only one thing happening today and he had zero interest in going.

Shaheer: That's the last place I wanna be
Zohra: Why? I thought you'd want to
Shaheer: Are you kidding? After the way he's been treating me?? Not a chance

Zohra: . . . wait. I'm talking about LMCC's grand opening. What are YOU talking about??

Shaheer drew back in surprise. He swiped to his calendar app and . . . yup. The new masjid's unveiling was this afternoon. How could he have forgotten?

Shaheer: Oh. I thought you meant the hockey game

There was a space of five minutes before Zohra's next reply.

Zohra: It's not so bad if you come to that either. Ashar would be over the moon

He highly doubted it, but it was funny how the tables had turned. Now Shaheer, not Zohra, was the one mad at Ashar.

Shaheer: Thanks, but no thanks. I'm packing
Zohra: Packing?? For what?
Shaheer: Moving. My dad ended up getting the Missouri job. We leave tomorrow

Shaheer could feel Zohra's shock permeating through the screen. Their text thread came to a complete pause. He distracted himself by combing through what was left hanging in his closet. Fifteen minutes after he sent his last message, Zohra finally typed back.

Zohra: So . . . you're officially leaving?
Without even saying goodbye?

She sounded like she was accusing him. Shaheer swallowed hard. He didn't know what to say that would make it hurt less. To make any of them feel better.

Shaheer: Yeah. It's for the best
Zohra: Well. You should still go to the grand opening. You helped a lot. None of us will be there since that's when the big game is and we're all going to watch.

Regret sank in Shaheer's stomach. The thought of nobody showing up to support the new masjid made him unbearably sad. Most of their main volunteers would either be at the Husky Bladers versus Cardinal Jetters game with their parents or playing in it. Yeah, it was an unlucky coincidence, but it was just one day, Shaheer convinced himself. It didn't mean the masjid would stay empty or that the community would neglect it. When people were free, they'd visit. It just wouldn't be on the grand opening.

But no matter how many times he told himself that, Shaheer knew it wasn't true. *Our strength lies in our numbers.* Shaheer was one person. He couldn't be a symbol of strength for the entire community, but Zohra was right. Shaheer did play a big role. He had owned that project before he stopped participating once Dad announced they were taking off again.

And Shaheer was not okay with letting all his hard work go to waste. For once, he wanted to see something through. He wanted to see the result with his own eyes, even if it was just one time. Plus, he wouldn't have to worry about running into Mom or Ayoub Mamou there, since they'd be at the ice hockey game.

Yeah. You're right. Think I'll go, he told Zohra. She sent him a thumbs-up emoji right away.

Shaheer went in search of Dada and found him sprawled on the couch, one arm thrown over his face with a glass tasbeeh between his fingers. Shaheer nudged his side with one finger. "Dada?"

"Hngh?" Dada moaned.

"Can you take me to the Leesburg Muslim Community Center?" asked Shaheer. "It's too far for me to bike."

Dada dropped his arm and looked at him funny. "Come again?"

Shaheer touched the back of his head with one hand sheepishly. "The grand opening's today, and I helped—well, I mean, when we were switching places—I was one of the volunteers who helped set it up and I want to see how it turned out. Maybe we can catch an Uber?"

Dada stared at Shaheer like he'd made the most interesting discovery in the world. "We don't need to call an Uber."

"But the car's not here—"

"Yes, it is." Dad materialized from his bedroom, recently shaved and wearing a striped sweater and jeans. "I'll take us."

Shaheer startled. "You didn't go in for your last day of work?" he said, forgetting that they technically weren't speaking.

"I called in today."

"Why?" Dad never took random days off.

Dad shrugged. "I'm good at ignoring problems in every part of my life except work," Dad said. "With being a doctor, if I don't like a particular boss, or my schedule, or the hospital environment, I jump ship. But I can't quit being a father. I don't want to. There's no point in being in a respectable position if I can't make things right with my own son. The way he wants."

Shaheer locked eyes with Dad. Dad's jaw was set determinedly in a way that eerily reminded him of Ashar. It made a small smile escape Shaheer, which Dad took as a good sign.

Shaheer trod over to the coat closet and pulled his jacket on at the front door. "Then what are we waiting for? Let's go."

Dad grabbed his keys off the counter. "I did say I wanted to pay a visit to the masjid again. Doesn't hurt to start now."

"Oh, all right. Make me get up." Dada sat up exaggeratedly, but Shaheer noticed a smile creeping onto his face.

"Wear a hat," Shaheer said. "It's starting to get cold."

Dad grinned like he found Shaheer telling them to bundle up amusing. "So, you've been helping to decorate the masjid, huh? Are you any good at it?"

"I'll let you be judge of that." And because they were Dad and Shaheer, they didn't have to say anything else.

For the first time in a long time, Dad didn't feel so far away. It felt like he was really trying. That he wanted to be what Shaheer needed. There was a lot that was still left unsaid, and it might take them a while to sift through it. Shaheer would be ready for that day, but for now, the air was clear.

28
ASHAR

Ashar downed an entire energy drink while listening to Sohaib's pregame spiel. Unfortunately, it didn't help to untie the knot in his stomach.

"Remember. We stick to the plan," Sohaib concluded. "We've practiced it a hundred times. No surprises." He directed that last one at Ashar for good measure. Ashar was too tired to care about being singled out. He thought the whole "calculated move" thing slowed him down, but whatever Sohaib wanted, he guessed. Ashar didn't want to be the weak link. Not when the Icecaps coach would be in the stands watching them today.

Ashar was feeling good about his chances of getting into Arlington Academy after taking the exam that morning. All he needed to do now was play well and prove himself on the rink and he could very well be an Icecap next year.

The energy buzzing from Ashar's team forced him to clear his head of math, science, and reading comprehension. The Arlington exam was over now. He'd tried his best. Now it was time to be a Blader.

"Those punks always pull a fast one on their opponents," Daniel said. Except he used a much worse word than *punk*. Coach Taylor let it slide. "It's almost like they know what their teammates are gonna do before they do it. And their goalie's a legend." He let the weight of his words settle on the group. Defeating the Cardinals would mean they had a shot at making state regionals, too. It was a major game for all of them.

Jamal snorted. "We can take 'em. They're not *that* good. They've lost before and they'll lose again!"

After some parting words of his own, Coach Taylor told them it was time to go, and they filed out of the locker room feeling invigorated. Ashar, Eddie, and Ramiz brought up the rear.

Outside the locker room, Ashar was hit by a blast of cold air that knocked his senses awake. If it hadn't, he probably wouldn't have noticed Zohra standing right outside, looking like she'd been waiting for him.

"Hey, why aren't you sitting with everyone else?" he asked her.

"I have to tell you something," she said. Underneath her green beanie, Zohra's cheeks were slightly tinged from the chilled air. She stepped closer to Ashar so that only he could hear the next part. "It's about Shaheer."

Ashar's nerves zipped. He could tell by Zohra's expression that this was crucial, otherwise she wouldn't have intercepted him right before the game.

"I'll catch up with you guys in a sec," Ashar called to Eddie and Ramiz.

"Make it quick," said Eddie.

Ashar directed his attention back to Zohra. "What's up?"

"I talked to Shaheer this morning," she said. "Your dad took the job in Missouri." Zohra's shoulders fell. "Ashar, they're leaving."

The room, the crowd noise, it all disappeared. *Leaving.* Ashar's whole world slanted on that one word. It sounded like it was set in stone. Heat rose in his face. Why did Zohra have to tell him this right before the biggest game of his entire life? He couldn't afford any distractions that would get in the way of him playing his best!

Leaving? The horrible truth knocked Ashar off

balance. Because of what he'd said to Shaheer at the airport! *Stupid! You're so stupid!*

"Listen," Zohra said, pulling Ashar out of his downward spiral. "Shaheer's going to be at the Leesburg masjid's grand opening today. He told me he would."

Ashar didn't have to ask Zohra why she was mentioning this to him. "When's that?"

"Uh, soon. Like right now."

No. He couldn't miss the Cardinals game. It was impossible. He'd worked his tail off for the Arlington exam. He couldn't sit out when he'd already made it this far! Ashar needed to get his head in the game if he was going to dominate out there. This was the important part. He couldn't think about Shaheer right now. His whole future was riding on his playing.

"I know it's not possible. I know becoming an Icecap is everything to you, but I thought—" She stopped. Zohra looked like she physically couldn't keep talking.

"You go," said Ashar. "It's okay, you don't have to stay here."

Zohra shook her head. "It wouldn't be the same." Ashar knew Zohra didn't say that to make him feel bad, but it stung anyway to know that he was letting her down.

Shaheer was her cousin, too, and she didn't want him to leave any more than he did. Zohra could probably tell by the way Ashar kept anxiously looking down the hall at the rink that this was a lost cause.

"Well," Zohra sighed. "Just thought I'd let you know. Good luck. You're gonna crush it out there." She fist-bumped Ashar in the shoulder, smiling sadly, then turned and ran back to her seat with the rest of their family.

Not their entire family, though.

Ashar stood there outside the locker room alone for what felt like hours. Then he took a deep, steadying breath, trying to focus. Because if he didn't, he'd be the one *getting* crushed. Ashar lowered his helmet cage, caught up to the rest of his team, and sprang onto the ice when the ref blew the whistle.

✦ ✦ ✦

The Cardinals players were in red, white, and black. For some reason they looked huge, even though the players on both teams were the same age.

The ref dropped the puck to officially commence the game, and the players scattered like red and purple ants as Sohaib and the Cardinals' center fought for control of the puck. Sohaib won, shooting the puck straight into the Cardinals' defensive zone for Daniel and Jamal to receive with open arms.

The feeling of being on the ice brought some clarity to Ashar's senses. He stayed in position behind the blue-line boundary of his team's defensive zone while Eddie moved more freely to pitch in with offense. Ashar was glad he'd been instructed to take few risks and focus on defending against the Cardinals' forwards, but that meant he wouldn't get an opportunity to score. Whatever. He could hold their ground just as well.

Ten minutes into the first period, Ashar was reminded of why the Cardinals were a big deal. They were insanely good. Their players were excellent skaters, specifically when it came to speed. Ashar's vision blurred red at times trying to keep up with them. One of the Cardinals' defensemen committed a minor penalty and was ordered to sit out for two minutes. The Bladers took advantage of that and passed back and forth until Jamal made the game's first goal. A cheer went up from the home stands.

The first period ended on a good note, with their side leading 2 to 1. Ashar hadn't had to do much except block a few shots and force away a Cardinal wingman who had rushed over to their side with the puck. During the fifteen-minute break, he sat on the bench and squirted some water in his face.

"You good?" Jamal asked Ashar.

"Mhmm," Ashar said. Sohaib was giving pointers based on what they'd seen so far, but Ashar barely heard him. He was too busy staring at the clock, his mind turning cloudy. This might be the only chance he had to run after Shaheer. If he didn't, Ashar might never see him again. He still might never see him again, but at least Ashar would know that he tried to prove to Shaheer that he mattered to him. Shaheer was probably already at the grand opening. Suddenly, it was too hard for Ashar to breathe. His judgment started twisting. Maybe he should—

Wait a minute. Why was he even thinking that? His team needed him here. He couldn't stand the thought of abandoning his post. Not when the Icecaps coach was watching them from the stands and cataloging every play of all the best players. Plus, none of the others were as familiar with coordinating defense with Eddie as he was. They could practically read each other's minds.

One wrong move could cost them the whole game, and Ashar didn't want to be that one wrong move.

"Ashar, did you hear?" Sohaib asked, breaking him out of his funk.

"Yeah," Ashar replied automatically, even though he hadn't.

When the second period started and they went back out there, Ashar was even more keyed up than before.

Ashar swayed on his feet, exhaustion hanging over his head like a dark cloud about to unleash at any minute. His gear suddenly felt like it weighed a thousand pounds. He couldn't even make out who had the puck now, or track what his teammates were doing. Why were Daniel and Sohaib shouting? Where had Eddie gone? What was the plan again?

"Ash! Ashar! He's headed your way!" Sohaib shouted at him. He spun back around and caught a glimpse of a Cardinal with huge shoulders barreling right at him with the puck. In a last-ditch effort, Ashar skated a few feet backward to make some attempt at covering Ramiz in the net.

That was when the Cardinal sent a slapshot at their goal and Ashar's world . . . slowed. Time moved at a snail's pace. For a split second, he couldn't make sense of anything. Then, through the slowly clearing haze, Ashar absorbed every detail of his surroundings. There was the puck veering low and to his side. There were Bladers and Cardinals stationed around him on the ice. There was Coach Taylor and the Icecaps coach staring right at him outside the rink to see what he would do. His family cheering for him on the bleachers.

But someone was missing.

Ashar's own words echoed back to him from his memory. *You know what would really suck, even more than me not getting into Arlington and getting to play for the Icecaps? Never seeing you again.*

And that was the moment he knew. Ashar could stay here and keep playing and bag a victory. But then he'd be a twin without a twin. He might win the game, but he would lose his brother.

He wasn't going to let that happen.

Ashar swung left and the puck cleared him. He sprinted off the ice like his life depended on it. A wave of dissent went up from several different people on his team.

"Malik!" Coach Taylor shouted incredulously. He'd gone extremely white. "What do you think you're doing?"

"Sorry, Coach!" Ashar said as he made a beeline for the exit. "I'll make it up to you later!"

Once he was off the ice, Ashar's whole family rushed down to meet him.

"Ashar," Mom said, sounding worried. "What's happening?"

Ashar removed his helmet and mouth guard. He felt so much lighter, but urgency still nipped at his heels. "Mom. The Leesburg masjid. We need to go there. Right now."

Mom and Ayoub Mamou traded a confused look. "Why? You still have half the game left," said Ayoub Mamou.

"I know." Ashar glanced at Zohra. She had tears in her eyes. Ashar looked away fast before they transferred to him. "But Shaheer's at the grand opening and I . . . have to see him. I need to make things right. It can't wait. I've already wasted a lot of time."

Mom rubbed his shoulder. "But honey, this game is so important to you."

Ashar looked straight at Mom and said in his most confident voice, "Not as important as my brother." Everyone stared at him with a mix of marvel and . . . something else. Ashar ignored the noise from the stands and the furious movement on the rink, his heart smashing around in his chest. Would they just think he was acting recklessly? Mom dropped her hand. Understanding and what looked like pride shone on her face. She nodded.

"So, will you guys help me?" asked Ashar.

29
SHAHEER

The turnout at the Leesburg Muslim Community Center was better than Shaheer had expected, but it was still a small gathering. The outside looked way better than the last time Shaheer had seen it, with a fresh coat of paint, new windows, and recently cut grass. He couldn't wait to see how it had turned out inside.

Imam Khalid led the ribbon-cutting ceremony with a short dua, then launched into a speech about the importance of tying oneself to the masjid and how they should all be generous with their time and donations. Shaheer stood in the parking lot with Dad and Dada flanking him on either side. Imam Khalid reminded Shaheer of Sohaib and the game happening on the other side of town, and Sohaib made Shaheer think of Ashar. He wondered how the Husky Bladers were faring against the Cardinals.

"And now," Imam Khalid said from the porch, "I'd like to take a few minutes to recognize the volunteers who contributed significantly to LMCC's renewal. Without them, none of this would have been possible. A special thanks goes to—"

HONNKKK!

Shaheer almost peed his pants as the loud sound sent a shock wave through the peaceful gathering. Two cars swerved off the road and drove onto the masjid's property, then came to jerky stops next to the group in front of the building. Someone blared the horn again.

"What in God's name do these people think they're doing?" Dada murmured. There were some nervous whispers around them.

Shaheer leaned past Dad to get a good look at who had crashed the party. He couldn't believe it when he recognized whose cars they were.

Zohra jumped out first, waving her hands wildly above her head. She was followed by her parents. Then Ashar and Mom emerged from the second car. The five of them lined up before the crowd like superheroes who'd just arrived in the nick of time. Zohra gave Shaheer a wide smile. It had been so long since Shaheer had talked to Zohra face-to-face that seeing her pink hair and glasses up close again hit him with nostalgia.

Zohra ran up to him, her parents tailing her more hesitantly from behind.

"You came?" Shaheer said, amazed. "And you brought them, too?"

"It wasn't just me," Zohra said, hooking her thumb over her shoulder at Ashar. She wiggled her fingers at Dad and Dada like she'd known them for ages.

"Assalamualaikum," Dada said. "Zohra, right? My, you've grown so big."

Ayoub Mamou nodded curtly at Dad. "Jawad."

"Ayoub," said Dad. "It's been a long time."

"Uncle," Ayoub Mamou said more nicely to Dada. "How is your health?"

"Alhamdulillah. I'd prefer more hair, improved eyesight, and a better back, but you know." Dada shrugged. "In other words, never better."

Ayoub Mamou and Faiza Mami laughed. Trust Dada to lighten the mood.

Not able to help himself, Shaheer threw his arms around his uncle. Ayoub Mamou stumbled in surprise but returned the embrace doublefold once he got his bearings.

"My boy." His voice was a whisper, a prayer, and hope all wrapped up in one. "You came home."

"Shaheer?"

Shaheer blinked fast at the voice and slowly turned. Mom was striking in a long coat, her hair pinned back. She glanced briefly at Dad before fixating on Shaheer. Her eyes gobbled him up, eyes that Shaheer only just now realized were the same dark brown as his and Ashar's.

The other adults' polite conversation stalled when they noticed Mom and Dad staring at each other wordlessly. Mom wrung the gloves in her hands and pretended to smile at Dad.

"What are you doing here?" he asked her.

"I'm here for my son," Mom said, forcing the same air of casualness as him.

Shaheer finally looked at Ashar, the sight of him stirring unwelcome feelings inside him. Ashar was wearing his purple Bladers jersey. "Did you win?" Shaheer asked.

"Dunno," said Ashar. "We left early."

Shaheer's mouth opened in surprise. "You what? Why would you do that?" He knew how much ice hockey meant to Ashar and what was at stake for him. Arlington Academy. The Icecaps. The NHL. What made him give all that up? How could he be so reckless?

Ashar came up to Shaheer slowly, like he was afraid of scaring him away. Time stopped and they descended into complete silence as Ashar held his breath and Shaheer waited.

"For you," Ashar confessed softly. "I came for you. To tell you that I'm sorry."

"You wouldn't talk to me," Shaheer rasped out. "Wouldn't even look at me for weeks! And now you skipped the big game to come here and *apologize*?" Ever since Shaheer had met Ashar, he'd wished he had even a sliver of his drive and confidence. But he didn't think this was Ashar's brightest moment.

"Yes," Ashar said. "Because you're worth it. I don't want to lose my brother, and I wanted him to know that before it was too late."

The space between them constricted until it felt like they were looking at each other—*really* looking at each other—for the first time. Ashar put his hands on Shaheer's shoulders. It was as if Ashar's touch coupled with his words punched a hole in Shaheer's resolve. Tears welled in his eyes. And in that moment, Shaheer realized that sometimes confidence wasn't always about making the big bold decisions or mouthing off to people. Sometimes confidence looked like the quiet strength it took to tell someone how much they meant to you.

Without a second thought, Shaheer folded Ashar into his arms, and Ashar's muscles tensed in surprise. When he finally processed that Shaheer. Was. Hugging. Him! Ashar crushed him in return, like this moment was the only thing holding him together. They remained locked that way, unmoving and unspeaking, until Dad gathered them against him. He rested his cheek on top of Ashar's head.

"I wasn't strong enough for the two of you," Dad said, choking up. "I'm sorry. For not reaching out. For letting you down. Your mom raised an incredible, hardworking boy. I only wish I'd been around to see you grow up. Together." Each syllable felt like Dad trying to clean out his soul. "I want to stay right here with both of my sons, if Zareena will let me."

Shaheer and Ashar looked at Mom and Dad expectantly. Instead of fever-pitch hate, there was a tolerant coolness between their parents when they locked eyes. Like ice melting. A truce.

"Yes," Mom finally said. "I want that, too. There was no excuse for what we did. I can't change the past, but if you still want me around, I'll spend the rest of my life making it up to you."

Shaheer swallowed the burning sensation in his

throat. "Of course I want you around, Mom," he said. "I just needed to know that you felt the same way."

Mom bent her head down a little until their eyes met. There wasn't a huge height difference between them. In a year or two, Ashar and Shaheer would catch up to her, maybe even outgrow her. "More than anything. I know Ashar does, too."

Shaheer scooted closer and leaned his forehead against her. Mom took Shaheer's hand and squeezed, sending Shaheer countless little apologies through their clasped fingers. For a moment, it was like it was just the four of them. Everything and everyone else melted away in the background and he, Ashar, Mom, and Dad existed in their own little bubble. Something clicked into place inside Shaheer, and he couldn't place what it was right away.

Ashar fell against Dad, sniffling quietly. Dada gave Shaheer a thumbs-up and Shaheer smiled at him over Dad's shoulder.

"Well, I think this calls for celebration," Ayoub Mamou said with a big grin. "Let's open a masjid! Take it away, Imam Khalid!"

Imam Khalid cleared his throat, but he was clearly pleased. "As I was saying earlier. One person devoted a lot of time to this project. His suggestions went a long way to making this masjid feel like the welcoming home we envisioned for this community. That's why I would like to thank Ashar Malik—"

"Nope!" Ashar yelled through cupped hands. "That wasn't me! That was my brother, Shaheer Atique, the greatest interior designer of all time!"

"Shaheer Atique," Imam Khalid said. "May Allah give you bountiful blessings for your labor of love."

Shaheer blushed extra hard when the other attendees chorused, "Ameen!" Imam Khalid cut the ribbon, and the cheers and clapping intensified. Inside, everyone examined the new space like it was a museum. A painted mural of the Kaaba against a colorful background graced one entire wall. It was the most beautiful masjid Shaheer had ever seen, and it was all *his*.

"Everyone is welcome at our place for dinner afterward," Ayoub Mamou said, looking pointedly at Dad and Dada. "If you would like to join us."

"Who can say no to an invitation like that?" asked Dada, winking at Shaheer and Ashar while Zohra squealed, jumping up and down.

Shaheer closed his eyes and took a deep breath. He was finally able to place what he'd felt outside. A sense of belonging. He looked around at everyone—Mom, Dad,

Dada, Ashar, Zohra, Ayoub Mamou, Faiza Mami—and felt peace at what he found. Shaheer could've been anywhere in the world, but he knew as long as he had his people, it didn't matter where he was.

They were his Forever Home. At long last.

30
ASHAR

"Okay, guys. Let's settle this once and for all. Who's older?" asked Ashar.

"Shaheer," Mom said from the dining table. "By six minutes." Shaheer stuck his tongue out at Ashar playfully.

They were all at Mom and Ashar's house for dinner after Zohra's winter band concert. Dada, Shaheer, Ashar, and Zohra were playing ludo in the family room. Over chai, Mom, Dad, Ayoub Mamou, and Faiza Mami were discussing some family gossip that had trickled down to them from New Jersey. Ashar had tried explaining to Shaheer their various distant cousins and other extended family who they rarely saw except at weddings. Shaheer seemed less interested in meeting them by the minute.

"Who cares? I'm still older than both of you," Zohra said, rolling the dice on her turn.

Dada made a noise in the back of his throat. "I'm older than the three of you combined. I win."

"Actually, I do." Zohra pushed her last red token into the finishing square and did a little dance.

"This game's rigged," Shaheer complained, sitting back against the sofa and crossing his arms. "There's no way you always win."

Usually, Ashar would gripe at losing, too, but he'd been in a good mood since Mom got the email yesterday about him being an Arlington semifinalist. Now all he needed to do was make it through the final evaluation process, which included an essay and teacher recommendations. He still didn't know what his chances were at joining the Icecaps after he'd bailed on the big Cardinals game, but Coach Taylor assured Ashar he didn't have to worry about it.

"I'll speak with Coach Werner," Coach Taylor said after Ashar had explained himself. Even learning about Ashar's twin and the fact that he'd been taking Ashar's place at a few practices so that he could study for the Arlington entrance exam with Dad didn't crack Coach Taylor's facade. What a weird dude. "Life happens."

While Ashar was relieved, this did mean that he and Shaheer would end up going to different high schools if he got in. But at least they would be in each other's lives. Mom and Dad had their ups and downs, but the overall arrangements they'd come up with worked for everyone. While Shaheer was still primarily at Dad's and Ashar was at Mom's, they were free to go to either house whenever they felt like it, and everyone had dinner together once a week. They didn't have it all figured out yet, but it was a start.

Ashar knew Mom and Dad struggled to stay civil sometimes, but they were trying. That was all that mattered. Dad had turned down the Missouri job to stay nearby, and checked up on Ashar often, which pleased Mom. He'd even bought Ashar extra hockey gear, assuring Mom it was a gift and not him trying to undermine her. It was going to come in handy for the last couple of games. The Husky Bladers had defeated the Cardinals without him, and their ranking had gone up. With any luck, Ashar would graduate from middle school on one of the top teams. They were not the NHL-bound Icecaps, but they were *his* team. And that was good enough for Ashar.

Dada went to join the other adults at the table, leaving

the three of them to put the game back. Shaheer placed the lid back on the box and returned it to its rightful drawer. Ashar admired his brother's hard work. Shaheer had taken their plain rental property and, with Mom's and Ashar's help, turned it into a place made for joy. Shaheer's handprints were everywhere, as they should be. Shaheer called it an "inviting space." He was starting to get into DIY, too. He'd pulled Ashar into a few of his projects, which Ashar didn't really enjoy as much as spending time with his brother.

Ashar, Shaheer, and Zohra drank their hot chocolate around the coffee table, talking about eighth-grade field day in the spring and what courses they were going to take next year since they had to start thinking about that stuff now. Ashar didn't miss the excitement in Shaheer's voice, like they were staying up late the night before Eid. This was his brother's first time talking about the future without fearing that it would go up in smoke, and Ashar's heart twinged happily. Whenever they were together, it felt like there'd never been a gap. Like it had always been the three of them. The rest of their family might've been an unfinished puzzle, but he, Zohra, and Shaheer fit perfectly.

In the middle of their conversation, Zohra looked out the window and gasped. "Snow!" she exclaimed.

Shaheer and Ashar jumped to their feet excitedly and rushed toward the deck, ignoring their parents telling them to put on jackets. The late January night was biting, but Ashar, Shaheer, and Zohra didn't care as they watched snowflakes drift down from the sky and kiss their faces. The deck was already covered in a layer a half inch thick.

"Finally," Ashar said, his breath loosing in pale puffs. "I was afraid we'd miss out this year. I need a snow day stat."

"You totally learned that word from Dad. And you guys get snow days?" Shaheer asked in wonder. His dark hair and lashes were already spattered with white dots. "Everywhere I've lived, they never gave us the day off."

"And yet another reason why Virginia's the best," said Ashar.

Shaheer's mouth turned up at one corner, and Ashar was sure few things in the world were better than his twin's smile, however sarcastic. "Yeah," Shaheer agreed. "Just one more to add to the list." Ashar gave Shaheer a wide, adoring puppy-dog gaze and his brother rolled his eyes. "I didn't mean you. Cut the ego."

"Literally, Ash," Zohra said, catching snowflakes in her upturned palm. "You're not that special."

"Ouch. Where's the loyalty?"

"I got your loyalty right here." Confused, Ashar turned

to Shaheer just as he pelted him in the face with a snow-ball. Ashar reared back in surprise. Zohra laughed and high-fived Shaheer.

Ashar frowned as bits of ice slid down his face. "What was that for?"

"Let's see how good you are with ice when you're not skating on it," Shaheer goaded him, wiggling his fingers at his sides.

Zohra cupped her hands in front of her mouth and chanted, "Fight, fight!" loud enough for the neighbors to hear.

Oh, so that's how it was going to be. Fine. Ashar never said no to a challenge, even if it came from his own brother.

And besides, he thought as he prepared to give Shaheer a taste of his own medicine, a little recklessness never hurt anybody.

ACKNOWLEDGMENTS

It's true what they say—second books are hard, and *Bhai for Now* was made even harder for being my "pandemic" book. Ashar and Shaheer's story carried me through some big life-changing events, but through it all, I found solace in their company. I have many others to thank for going on this journey with me:

My agent, Lauren Spieller, for embracing this story from the get-go. You are still the best advocate for my books that I could have ever asked for. Thank you for what you do every day.

My editor, Emily Seife. Thank you for not dropping me when I sent you the horrible first draft, for gently guiding me through revisions, and for your patience as I revised through third trimester/Ramadan/postpartum. Also, for coming up with the perfect title. I'm so grateful that I had the chance to work with you again. All my love to Taylan Salvati, Elisabeth Ferrari, Janell Harris, and the rest of my Scholastic family for everything they do to bring my books in front of readers and for giving Ashar and Shaheer a warm welcome.

To Javeria M. Talha for nailing yet another cover illustration! And Omou Barry for tying it all together with the most perfect design. Thank you for bringing Ashar and Shaheer to life.

To Aya Khalil, Reem Faruqi, and Saadia Faruqi for your wisdom and words of encouragement. But above all else, for your friendship. You all inspire me every day.

Thank you, Lauren Blackwood, for introducing me to our ambrosia. I drank way too much of it to survive revisions, but it was worth it!

To Tom Harvey, for answering all my burning questions about ice hockey. All mistakes in this book regarding the sport are my own.

Thank you to my family—immediate and extended— for putting up with me through my debut year and for being excited about my second book before I'd even finished writing it.

To my parents for always being there for me even when I don't deserve it.

My brothers. You guys did nothing special except give me inspiration to write a story about two brothers who— despite their differences—are better together. Your bond is the one thing I've always envied about you. You do *one* thing right, I guess.

To my husband, Usman, and my mother-in-law for their endless support in taking over the house and kids and literally turning their own schedules upside down and inside out so that I could do revisions—twice. I will never be able to repay you.

And lastly, as always, thank you, Allah (SWT), for the chance to tell another story, and hopefully more in the future. Because even if I stop believing in myself, I never stop believing in You.

ABOUT THE AUTHOR

MALEEHA SIDDIQUI is an American writer of Pakistani descent who loves to tell stories for all ages about the American Muslim experience. She can't live without caffeine, rainy days, and books with a whole lot of heart. Her debut novel, *Barakah Beats*, was an ABA Indies Introduce pick. By day, Maleeha works as a regulatory affairs professional in the biotech industry. She grew up and continues to reside with her family in Virginia. Find her at maleehasiddiqui.com and on Twitter and Instagram at @malsidink.